ORLAND PARK PUBLIC
31315 00514 4089
W9-BNU-063

THE STONE CHILD

THE STONE CHILD

Dan Poblocki

RANDOM HOUSE NEW YORK

Published in the United States by Random House Children's Books,
a division of Random House, Inc., New York.

Random House and the colophon are registered trademarks of Random House, Inc.

Visit us on the Web! www.randomhouse.com/kids

Educators and librarians, for a variety of teaching tools,
visit us at www.randomhouse.com/teachers

Library of Congress Cataloging-in-Publication Data
Poblocki, Dan.
The stone child / Dan Poblocki. — 1st ed.
p. cm.
Summary: When friends Eddie, Harris, and Maggie discover that the scary adventures in their favorite author's fictional books come true, they must find a way to close the portal that allows evil creatures and witches to enter their hometown of Gatesweed.
ISBN 978-0-375-84254-2 (trade) — ISBN 978-0-375-94254-9 (lib. bdg.) —
ISBN 978-0-375-84255-9 (pbk.) — ISBN 978-0-375-85388-3 (e-book)
[1. Authors—Fiction. 2. Books and reading—Fiction.
3. Supernatural—Fiction. 4. Monsters—Fiction.] I. Title.
PZ7.P7493St 2009
[Fic]—dc22
2008021722

Printed in the United States of America
10 9 8 7 6 5 4 3 2 1
First Edition

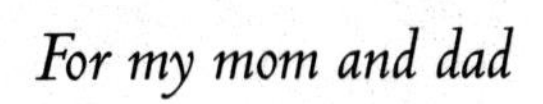
For my mom and dad

THE STONE CHILD

1

The blue station wagon had just come around a sharp bend in the road when the creature stepped out of the woods. Eddie was the first to see it—a blur of black hair and four long, thin legs. It looked at him with red-rimmed yellow eyes and a gaping mouth full of sharp teeth.

"Watch out!" Eddie cried from the backseat.

His father smashed his foot against the brake pedal. The car began to fishtail; the tires squealed. Eddie felt himself jerk forward against the seat belt as several of the boxes stacked on the backseat of the car tumbled onto the floor beside him. The book he had been reading flew out of his hands and smacked against the seat in front of him. Eddie's mother clutched at the ceiling and let out a yelp. Then came the horrible crunch as the front of the car crashed into the creature, sending it flying into the greenish darkness of the woods.

The right side of the car skidded off the road and shuddered over several small shrubs, before lurching to a stop a few feet from a mossy boulder. Through the windshield, Eddie watched steam hiss from underneath the car's mangled hood.

"Is everyone all right?" asked Eddie's father after several seconds of stunned silence. Eddie had to think about that—his shoulder burned where the seat belt had caught him. He felt like he'd had his breath knocked out of him—partly because of what he'd seen step in front of the car. Its horrible face was lodged in his mind.

"I'm okay," said Eddie's mother.

"Me too," Eddie managed to say.

"I'm so sorry," said Eddie's father. "I didn't even see it coming."

"Look at the front of the car," said Eddie's mother, removing her seat belt. "How could a deer do so much damage?"

"Too big for a deer . . . I think it was a bear," said Eddie's father, leaning forward over the steering wheel, peering into the trees where the animal had disappeared. He opened his door.

The car sat at the top of an incline, hugging the curve of the wooded, winding road. "Stay inside," said Eddie suddenly. He was certain the thing had been neither a deer nor a bear. His father looked at him like he was crazy. "Drive away," Eddie insisted.

"I need to see the damage. The moving trucks are probably already waiting for us at the new house."

"Yeah, but—"

"Edgar Fennicks, don't be ridiculous!" said Eddie's mother. "It's probably injured . . . or dead. Your father hit it really hard." His parents both got out of the car and closed their doors, leaving him alone in the backseat. They marched to the front of the car and examined the bumper. Eddie's father threw his hands into the air in frustration. His mother covered her mouth and turned away toward the woods. Eddie looked at the woods too. The foliage was dense, but other than the wind rustling the branches, there was no sign of movement in the area where the creature had landed.

Eddie didn't want to be alone. Reluctantly, he opened his door and stepped into the broken bushes.

It was the beginning of September, and the afternoon air was cool. From the top of the hill, Eddie could see the slate-gray sky hanging over the rolling hills like a tattered blanket. The only sound he heard was the wind through the trees. It sounded like someone whispering a secret. Maybe the thing was dead after all. The thudding sound the car had made when it hit the animal echoed in Eddie's head, giving him chills. He zipped up his blue hooded sweatshirt.

When he made it to the front of the car, he could see why his father was so upset. The right side had been crushed. The headlight was embedded in the front tire. Tufts of black hair were stuck to the crumpled metal. From the left side of the car, the bumper protruded like a broken bone. "Whoa," said Eddie. His parents merely shook their heads.

After a moment, Dad wandered back to the driver's-side door, got in, and started the car. "Watch it!" he called, shifting the gear into reverse. When he pressed the gas pedal, the axle cried out in a loud, piercing whine. He shook his head, turned the car off again, and grabbed his cell phone from the front seat.

As his father called the police, Eddie stood with his mother at the edge of the woods. She whispered, "Don't worry, Edgar. We're almost home."

"I'm not worried," said Eddie, even though he was, a little bit. His fingertips tingled, and the crunch of the metal resonated somewhere deep inside him. He would have been worried even if they hadn't just gotten into a car accident, but he figured it was normal to feel that way on the day you were moving to a new town. Everything was uncertain. After his mother had lost her office job in Heaverhill, she wanted a change of scenery. At the end of the previous school year, Eddie had said goodbye to his old classmates without knowing he might not see them again for a while. His parents had made the decision to move quite quickly. He had no idea what his new house would look like, or what his new classmates would be like. Eddie had been feeling pretty overwhelmed all day—all month, in fact—and so on the car ride down from Heaverhill, he'd been rereading one of his favorite books, *The Revenge of the Nightmarys.* Reading familiar stories was comforting, even stories as scary as the ones Nathaniel Olmstead had written. "Do you really think it's dead? Because . . . it looked like . . ."

"Like what?" said Mom.

"Like . . . a monster," said Eddie, "or . . . or something."

"A monster?" Mom laughed. "I wish my imagination were half as wild as yours, Edgar. I'd be a bestselling novelist by now."

"Didn't you see its face?"

"I didn't get a good look."

"Hey," called Eddie's father, "the cops are on their way with a tow truck. The officer I spoke with said we should probably wait inside the car."

"Why?" said Mom.

"I told him I hit a bear."

"What did you tell him that for?"

"Because it's true!"

"It *wasn't* a bear. It didn't look anything *like* a bear," she said, stepping back toward the car. "Edgar seems to think it was a monster. I swear, the two of you are such a pair."

Eddie was about to follow her back to the car, when something in the distance down the road caught his eye, freezing him where he stood. Across the dip of the next valley, where the road descended, Eddie noticed a simple box of a house sitting on top of a grass-covered hill. A patchwork of tall trees, the leaves of which were turning in the wind, surrounded the nearby hills. The smoky peaks of the Black Hood Mountains were visible on the horizon. He knew he'd seen this place before, but where? A postcard? A book? A dream? The familiarity of the sight was surreal enough to knock away the image of the creature his father had struck with the car. He wandered to the faded yellow line on the road for a better view.

A fat stone chimney, like an enormous gravestone, sprouted from the center of the house's pitched slate roof. Five small windows spread across the top floor. On the bottom were four windows framing a broken door twisting away from its hinges. Unpainted gray shingles peeled away from the sides of the house. Brush and bushes and weeds obscured the rest of the building.

His mouth went dry as he gasped. "No way," he whispered to himself, suddenly realizing where he'd seen the house.

"Edgar, you are going to get hit by a truck!" his mother called out the window from the passenger seat.

Eddie pointed at the hill. "But—"

"Come on," said his father, leaning out the driver's-side door. "Get in the car, bud."

Eddie stumbled to the car and climbed into the backseat.

"What were you looking at?" Mom asked. "Did you hear something in the woods? That thing's not still alive, is it?"

He didn't answer right away. Instead, he bent down and searched the floor for the book he'd been reading during the ride from Heaverhill. *The Revenge of the Nightmarys.* It was underneath his mother's seat.

"Edgar, what's wrong?" Mom said, peering at him from behind the blue vinyl headrest.

He opened the book's back cover and showed his parents the picture printed there. The man on the inside flap of the book jacket stood in front of a country house on top of a grassy hill. The windows were not broken. The weeds had not yet grown. The shingles were gray, and though they were not in perfect condition, they were in much better shape than the shingles on the house on the hill up the road. The fat stone chimney looked more like a monument than a gravestone, but still the resemblance was unmistakable. The man's face was serious, but his ruffled brown hair and short beard gave him the appearance of a kind, creative soul. Under his picture, a brief biography explained that *Nathaniel Olmstead lives in a small town in northwestern Massachusetts. He is an amateur astronomer, an ancient history buff, and a fan of monster movies.* When his parents finished looking at the picture, they stared at him, confused.

"Look . . ." Eddie pointed down the road.

"Hey!" said Dad, finally noticing the house on the hill.

Eddie had read somewhere that it had been empty for close to thirteen years, but it looked more like thirty.

"Isn't that odd . . . ?" said Mom.

"Is Gatesweed the town where Nathaniel Olmstead lived?" asked Eddie.

"I don't know," said Dad, distracted. "Who's Nathaniel Olmstead?"

"Dad! He's this guy!" Eddie pointed at the picture again. "He wrote all my favorite books. *The Revenge of the Nightmarys. The Wrath of the Wendigo. The Ghost in the Poet's Mansion. The Curse of the Gremlin's Tongue.* And tons more. Phantoms. Spirits. Creepy stuff like that."

"So *that's* why you thought you saw a monster in the road," said Mom, taking the book from him and examining the cover.

Eddie blushed. "Maybe."

"This Olmstead person couldn't possibly *still* live in that house," said Dad.

"Well, supposedly," Eddie said, "he disappeared, like, thirteen years ago. No one knows what happened to him, or whether he's even still alive. But his books are really popular. I've read all of them. At least twice."

"So his house is empty?" said Mom, glancing through the trees.

"Certainly looks empty," said Dad. "In that condition, who would live there?"

"I don't know," said Mom. "Possibly people stuck on this road come nightfall."

"Very funny," said Dad.

"Might be inspiring for someone who writes spooky stories," Eddie suggested.

"Yeah," said Dad, "if you don't use water or electricity, you could get *all* the inspiration you'd ever need."

A police car came speeding around the corner in front of them. It screeched to a halt next to Dad's car, facing the opposite direction. A frazzled old man in a wrinkled uniform sat behind the wheel. Long wisps of thin white hair struggled to hide his nearly bald head. His pinched eyes glared at them through thick glasses. He rolled down his window and motioned for Eddie's father to do the same. "You folks all right?" he said.

"We are, but the car's not," said Dad. "You want to take a look at it?"

"Uh-uh." The old man shook his head so hard his glasses went crooked. "Tow truck's comin'. He'll take care of you." He grabbed a clipboard from the passenger seat and held it through the window. A sheet of paper was attached to it. Eddie's father reached out through his own window and took it from him. "Fill this out for your insurance company. Drop it at the town hall when you get a chance."

"Well . . . ," said Dad, flustered, "I suppose I could just fill it out and give it to you now."

The old man shook his head again. "Tow truck'll be here soon. I can't wait around. . . . Got stuff to do." The police car shuddered as he put it into gear. Without saying goodbye, he rolled up the window and jerked his car up the road into a fast k-turn. When he had turned the police car around, he sped back down the hill.

Eddie's parents stared at each other. "Could he have gotten out of here any faster?" said Dad.

"Don't worry about him," said Mom, patting her husband's arm. "Remember when we came down for the house closing, honey? That nice woman we met in that pretty little bookstore said Gatesweed was peppered with eccentric people. All part of the charm, right?"

Through the windshield, Eddie watched the leaves in the forest flash white, their undersides whipped into a frenzy by the breeze. The trees parted and the house on the hill appeared again. It seemed to hold its breath, as if keeping a secret.

A few minutes later, a beat-up black tow truck rumbled into view behind the blue station wagon. A young guy, who looked to be in his late twenties, hopped out and sauntered up the road on the driver's side. He was tall and skinny. His tight black leather jacket was open, revealing a Metallica concert T-shirt. When he leaned toward Dad's open window, his scraggly black hair hung below his shoulders. Eddie could smell him from the backseat—a mixture of lingering cigarette smoke and vanilla air freshener. Eddie's parents cringed. The driver raised an eyebrow and smiled. "So . . . what did you hit?"

2

They all waited on the side of the road as the driver loaded the station wagon onto the tow truck's crane. Eddie's father explained what happened. The driver, who had introduced himself as Sam, listened, curious, nodding as Eddie's father told him how odd the police officer had been.

"Didn't even offer you a ride back into town?" asked Sam, opening the truck's passenger door for them. "That's Gatesweed for ya. Where you people from? Not around here, I bet."

Eddie thought the guy knew more than he was saying. He climbed into the truck and perched uncomfortably across his mother's and father's laps. Sam got behind the wheel. He turned the key, and the engine growled to life.

"We came down from Heaverhill," said Eddie's father. "Upstate New York. A few hours north."

"We're supposed to be moving in today," said Eddie's mother.

"Wait one wicked second. . . ." Sam turned his entire body to look at her. "You're moving *into* Gatesweed?"

"Well, yeah," said Mom, clutching her pocketbook to her chest. "Why?"

Sam sniffed and shook his head. "Nothing. It's just that when it comes to this town, most people move *out,* not in. My parents left when I was still in high school. I live across the Rhodes River Bridge, east of here."

"Parts of the town seem a little . . . *deserted,* sure," said Mom, "but overall, it's such a pretty place. Don't you think?"

Sam pulled onto the road. "Yeah. Right. Pretty." He turned on the radio. Heavy metal music rattled the broken speakers in the dashboard—the singer was screaming something about blood. "So it was Gatesweed's *abundant beauty* that lured you?" he asked with a smirk.

Out the window, Eddie watched as they passed a crooked iron fence on the left side of the road. Dead vines were wrapped around the rusty spikes, as if the woods were trying to drag the fence down into the dirt.

"Actually," said Dad, "that's sort of exactly right. . . . We drove out a few months ago for an antiques fair just north of the Black Hood Mountains, and my wife fell in love with the area. I'm an antiques dealer. . . . We thought Gatesweed might be a great spot for collecting new pieces. We started looking and almost immediately found a deal on a beautiful house with a big barn in the backyard. . . . Figured, what the heck? Perfect spot to store antiques. Perfect town for my wife to start writing again."

"You're a writer?" Sam asked Eddie's mother.

"Sort of. I haven't published anything yet," she said. "Speaking of writers, why don't you ask about that house, Edgar?" Eddie could tell she was trying to change the subject. He blushed, embarrassed that she was drawing attention to him. "My son wanted to know if the house back there belongs to that author . . . Nathaniel Olmstead?"

Sam was silent for almost five seconds. Finally, he answered. "Yeah, sure. It belongs to him . . . ," he said, before correcting himself, "or it *belonged* to him."

"Did you know him?" asked Dad.

"Not really. I saw him around every now and then when I was a kid," said Sam. "Quiet guy. If anyone knows what happened to him, they ain't talking. A mystery. Like something out of one of his books." Sam glanced at Eddie. "I read them all when I was your age. What are you, twelve?"

Eddie nodded.

"Yeah," Sam continued, "me and my friends were obsessed. Every time a new book came out, we would go around town looking for the places that Nathaniel Olmstead wrote about. Freak each other out and stuff."

"Wait," said Eddie, sitting up straight, "he wrote about places *in* Gatesweed?"

"Hell, yeah. The Devil's Tree on Mansion Street. The old church rectory. The wood mill bridge. The statue of Dexter August in the town green. They're all right here. His inspiration, they say. Me and my friends would hang out in these places at night. The cops used to bust us up. Said we were disturbing the peace . . . having too much fun. But that was before my friend Jeremy . . ." He turned the wheel sharply as the road curved to the right. He didn't finish his sentence.

"Before your friend Jeremy what?" asked Eddie.

The driver sucked his teeth. "You're an Olmstead fan. You must've heard the stories."

"What stories?" said Mom.

Sam chuckled, but he did not sound amused. "The Olmstead Curse . . ."

Olmstead Curse?

Eddie suspected that the words were supposed to scare him, but for some reason, he felt intrigued. He'd just learned that he was moving into the town where his favorite author had written all of his favorite books—and now this guy was talking about curses? A strange, nervous warmth was growing in his stomach. The way the weird old policeman had driven off and left them stranded suddenly seemed to make sense—the man was frightened to get out of his car. Was that because of this curse? Eddie wanted to tell Sam about the animal his father had hit, that it had looked like a monster, but he had a feeling his parents didn't want to hear any more about it.

Eddie shook his head.

"Oh, come on!" said Sam.

"No. I haven't heard of it," said Eddie.

"A curse?" said Eddie's father. "You can't be serious."

Sam didn't answer.

"What kind of curse is it?" Eddie's mother tried.

"I think I've already done enough damage to Gatesweed's reputation for one afternoon," said Sam. "I do sort of depend on this town for business. Can't go scaring you off, especially now that you live here. If you want to know more, you can look it up for yourself."

"You can't say something like that and then just leave it," said Eddie's mother, clutching her pocketbook even closer.

The truck came around a bend in the road. Several sharp-peaked roofs bit through the treetops ahead. Then, suddenly, the whole town appeared, cupped in the small circular valley beyond the lip of the hill.

"I'd offer to check under your bed tonight for ya," said Sam, turning up the radio, "but I don't want to intrude." The music shrieked and the windows of the small cab trembled. "Don't you just love this song?"

Sam took a right onto Heights Road. The truck rose up the steep hill, shuddering as it tried to shift gears. Eddie couldn't believe they were almost home. So much was happening so quickly.

Every house they passed might be the one where they would stop. Strange how so many of them looked empty. Their windows were dark, the glass broken. Most of the large front lawns were unkempt and overgrown, as if no one had touched them in years. As unbelievable as it seemed, maybe the driver had been right. Maybe everyone really *had* left Gatesweed.

Were curses real? Eddie wondered.

The long truck he had last seen in Heaverhill was parked in front of a quaint gray house at the top of the road. When the tow truck stopped, his father opened the door, and Eddie leapt from the cab onto the curb. He started to run up the driveway. He was nearly at the garage when he heard his father call, "Edgar!"

Eddie turned around and called back, "I need to find my books!"

3

Ronald could see his reflection on the lake's surface. The cold air bit through his thin jacket. Time was running out. He looked at the crumpled paper. It was difficult for him to read the writing. The moon had almost sunk beneath the horizon, and the light was fading. He needed to solve the riddle before the caretaker realized he'd torn the page from the mysterious book.

Ronald squinted to make out the position of the cross marks on the paper. He knew that the first × was the mansion itself, and he was pretty sure that the second × represented the statue of the girl in the clearing. But what location did the star represent? There were certainly plenty of stars reflected in the water, but which one held the answer to the question at the top of the page?

As he looked at the other shore, trying to notice another clue, the toes of his sneakers slipped forward and touched the wet, muddy edge of the lake, sending out tiny ripples. He immediately leapt backward. His grandfather had warned him—no matter what, do not touch the water.

Reflected in the water, some of the stars had already changed color, from white to red. As he watched, they all turned, then began to move. In an instant, they divided into hundreds of pairs of red eyes that watched him from under the lake's surface.

Ronald took a step backward and almost tripped as he turned to run. He made it to the woods before he heard the splashing.

"*Here* you are," said Mom.

Eddie sat on the dusty floor of the barn, surrounded by piles of boxes. Ronald Plimpton's story lingered in his mind's eye like smoke. Even after seeing his mother standing in the doorway, it still took him a moment to realize where he was. The orange overhead light bounced off the rafters above. The pitched roof of the barn was hidden in shadow. Outside, it was starting to get dark.

"I was looking all over for you," she said. "I'm gonna make dinner. Your father called. He'll be back from the garage in a few minutes. They gave him a loaner so he can drive himself home. . . . What are you doing in here?"

Once the movers had finished unloading the truck late that afternoon, Eddie had torn into the boxes they'd stacked in the barn. After seeing Nathaniel Olmstead's house on the hill and learning about the supposed curse from the tow truck driver, all Eddie had wanted to do was find his collection of books. Of course he'd read them all before, but, for a reason he couldn't quite name, Eddie needed to *have* them now. He wished he'd been more organized when he'd packed in Heaverhill. He'd forgotten to label some of his bedroom boxes. The movers had placed them in the barn with his father's antiques.

Eddie showed his mother the first book he'd found, the one he'd been reading when she'd interrupted. *The Rumor of the Haunted Nunnery.*

She pursed her lips. "Have you started on your bedroom at all? It's getting late."

Eddie shook his head. He couldn't concentrate on unpacking yet. This book had captured him again.

Mom had changed into a T-shirt and sweatpants to make the work of unpacking boxes more comfortable. It had been a long day. Leaning against the wooden door frame, she looked exhausted. "School starts the day after tomorrow, you know. You're not gonna have much more time to get organized before homework sets in." She suddenly looked closer at the book in his hands. "Hey, isn't that by—"

"Nathaniel Olmstead," said Eddie. "Ronald was about to run away from the monster lake-dogs."

"The monster lake-dogs?" said Mom. "Sounds scary."

"Once he makes it back to the mansion, he feeds them leftover chicken bones and escapes, so it all turns out okay," said Eddie.

"I never realized that leftover chicken bones worked so well at getting rid of monster lake-dogs."

"They're easily distracted," said Eddie, shrugging. "If you read the book, you'd know."

"Maybe I *should* read those books," said Mom. "I mean, if this town is cursed, I probably need to prepare myself." She rolled her eyes. "Can you believe that guy from the garage?" she said. "I was nervous to leave your father alone with him. Creepy."

Eddie laughed. "I thought he was sort of cool."

"Cool?" said Mom. "If serial killers are cool, then sure, that guy was very cool. Come on, let's go inside. You can help me find the pots and pans."

"But I wanted to find my books. They're all mixed up out here."

Mom sighed, glancing around at the mess. She nudged an open box with the toe of her boot. "Here . . . what about this one?" She reached inside and pulled out a leather-bound book. She tossed it to Eddie. He was surprised when he actually caught it.

Eddie had never seen it before. It was unlike the well-worn paperbacks for which he'd been searching.

The cover of the book was sturdy. The leather was tight but slightly worn around the edges. From the side, Eddie could see that the book was not thick, maybe 150 slightly yellowed pages. The gold lettering stamped directly onto the brown leather read *The Enigmatic Manuscript.* Despite its size, the book was heavy. When Eddie lifted the cover, it creaked, snapping at him as the old glue bent. Inside, Eddie found words scrawled in black ink in the center of the first page. When he read them, he gasped.

A story by Nathaniel Olmstead.

Underneath the author's name was a strange symbol.

Eddie didn't know what it was supposed to mean. "*The Enigmatic Manuscript*? What is this?" he said.

"Isn't it one of your books?" said Mom.

Shaking his head, Eddie held it open and showed it to her.

Realization washed across her face. "Oh," she said, "I remember now. . . . I picked up that book when your father and I came down for the Black Hood Antiques Fair a few months ago. I thought it looked interesting, like an old-fashioned artifact. We didn't know what it was, but your father thought it might be worth something. Isn't it odd Nathaniel Olmstead's name keeps coming up today?"

Odd is an understatement, Eddie thought. He suddenly felt as if this entire day could have been written by the missing author himself. A piece of the man seemed to be everywhere Eddie looked.

But the author's name on the first page was nothing compared to what was on the next page.

Eddie nearly dropped the book on the floor when he read:

VSP IYU POY PLY LDG UDM HUV HFP
WYF SYZ GYP FMG YHS PIY ZDU YFS
GDM RSF SYO DDG RPF YHK YYO VHD
LFS YIY GRY DTZ PFP HFG DAS YPL OVG
YPN VCY LDK FSP FVF VHU ETP MNF

Puzzled, Eddie flipped through all of the pages. He found the rest of the book to be the same: filled with three-letter, nonsense words. He showed the book to his mother. "What does it mean? Is it a sort of code or something?"

"Whatever it is," said Mom, heading back toward the house, "you've got a day to figure it out before school starts."

"Do you think Dad will mind if I hang on to it?"

"We'll ask him at dinner. If you do figure out what it means, he'll probably thank you. Especially if it *did* belong to this Olmstead person. Maybe it actually is worth something."

"Wow!" said Eddie. "This is so cool! Thanks!"

After dinner, Eddie's mother came upstairs to say good night. She kissed his cheek while he sat at his desk. "I'm going to try to write a little bit tonight, before I totally crash into pieces," she said. "I know it's been a long day, but try to organize your room before bed. Okay?"

"I'll try," Eddie said as she closed the door. "Good night."

Like the rest of the quaint bungalow, Eddie's new bedroom on the second floor was a mess. Empty boxes, crumpled pieces of newspaper, and piles of clothes littered the floor, a mess he'd managed to make since coming in from the barn. Much of the room lay beneath the tilt of the roof, but there was still plenty of space to stand. A gabled window with a southern view over the town cut into the sloping ceiling. The sun had set, and the sky was indigo.

Eddie picked up the book his mother had found in the barn. It smelled awful, like dirt or mold. Weird. He opened to the first page again. The strange symbol leapt out at him. Eddie placed the book onto his quilt and scrambled under his covers.

He reached out and ran his index finger down the spine of the book, feeling the impression of the title stamped vertically onto the cover. *A story by Nathaniel Olmstead*?

What if *The Enigmatic Manuscript* was in fact a handwritten Olmstead book? A new novel that no one had read before? It was possible. After all, his parents had found the book only a few towns away. Nathaniel Olmstead's name on the first page might actually be his signature! But if it was an unpublished novel, why would he have written it in a code language? Whatever the reason, Eddie was certain that there was something inside the book its author hadn't wanted anyone to know.

Eddie stared at the ceiling, his shoulder throbbing faintly where the seat belt had caught him. It had been such a weird day. Leaving his old house behind and driving from Heaverhill would have been unusual enough, but then his father had to go and hit that creature in the road.

Its gash of a mouth lolled open when Eddie shut his eyes for a moment. He shuddered and sat up, propping his pillows against his headboard.

After the accident, seeing the author's house and learning about the supposed Olmstead Curse only added to the day's peculiarity. Eddie knew that every town has its legends, but before he'd even had a chance to look around Gatesweed, it seemed as though, in a way, the spirit of Nathaniel Olmstead had come to haunt him. The funny thing was, Eddie didn't mind. Figuring out the book would be like exploring Nathaniel Olmstead's world, almost as if he were a character *inside* one of his stories. Plus, Sam had mentioned that Olmstead wrote about places in Gatesweed. Living here, Eddie could explore his world from the *outside* too!

Like the characters in Nathaniel Olmstead's books, Eddie had several questions: What exactly *is* the Olmstead Curse? Why do people move out of Gatesweed but not in? What exactly had happened to Jeremy, Sam's childhood friend?

This last question left Eddie feeling queasy instead of

excited, the way he felt about the others. Strangely, this third question was the one he was most afraid of answering.

Where should he begin?

Eddie looked down at the book in his lap.

In *The Rumor of the Haunted Nunnery,* Ronald found the key to decode a secret message. The message allowed Ronald to find the lake in the woods. Eddie knew Nathaniel Olmstead liked to include codes in his books. Could the writing in *The Enigmatic Manuscript* be one of those codes? If the town library had books about secret codes, maybe Eddie wouldn't need to find a key, like the one Ronald had discovered. Maybe Eddie could solve the code himself.

Shouldn't be too hard, he thought. After reading all of Nathaniel Olmstead's books several times, he'd become pretty good at figuring out stuff like this. One more day until school? Plenty of time, he thought with a smile.

4

After breakfast the next morning, Eddie begged his parents to let him explore the town. They agreed, but only after he had organized his closet, bureau, and desk. They also made him promise to be home for lunch.

Less than an hour later, he was out the door.

It was warm now that the sun had finally come out from behind the clouds. He didn't even need his hooded sweatshirt. Inside his backpack, he carried the two Olmstead books that weren't still packed away, as well as *The Enigmatic Manuscript.*

Standing next to his bike in the middle of his house's gravel driveway, Eddie had a perfect view of the town. The roads were laid out in concentric circles, linked by lanes and small side streets, like a labyrinth. A long, thin park divided the town in half. On the western end of the park, at the base of the surrounding hills, sat an old wooden church, and on the east, along the Black Ribbon River, huddled several mills.

He wished he'd been able to find the rest of his books the night before. He thought they might act as a map for his journey. Even though he could probably list certain places for which he should keep a lookout, like the ones Sam had mentioned yesterday, Eddie figured there must be hundreds of secret Gatesweed spots he'd never on his own think to look for. Then again, Eddie knew he had all the time in the world to explore Gatesweed. Right now, however, he had a mystery to solve.

The library had to be down there somewhere.

Heights Road wound down to the town center. Eddie's bike kicked up clouds of dust. Before he realized what he was doing, he'd sped by several empty houses, a few deserted storefronts, and a brick fortresslike town hall. He braked in front of the park, where the long grass rustled in the warm breeze. He was on Center Street. True to its name, it circled the center of the park and came back to the spot where Eddie stood.

Eddie glanced behind him, where an old movie theater sat quietly, the front of it blockaded haphazardly by a loose chain-link fence. When Eddie noticed the marquee over the entrance to the building, his skin went cold. He expected to see an old movie title hanging on the yellowed white panel, but instead, broken black letters spelled out strange words that reminded Eddie of the code from *The Enigmatic Manuscript.*

LO ED UN L FU HER NO ICE.

As he stared at the theater, Eddie realized he was wrong. The words were not part of any code—some of their letters were missing. Feeling like a contestant on a weird game show, Eddie slowly filled in the gaps.

CLOSED UNTIL FURTHER NOTICE.

The sign had fallen apart over time. Eddie suddenly felt entirely alone. The town seemed to be deserted.

Across from the park stood a wide brick building covered in ivy. Stone steps led up to a high arch, over which was carved GATESWEED PUBLIC LIBRARY. Near the roof, around the top of the cornice, more words decorated the building. A PLACE WHERE STORIES ARE TOLD. Eddie beamed.

Eddie had never had tons of friends. In Heaverhill, the kids didn't understand stuff like studying astrological star signs, or reading about old Babylonian statues, or researching ancient Aztec gods at the library. People in Heaverhill tended to ignore the way things could be or might have been, and so they tended to ignore Eddie. His mom was always trying to get him to talk to people. Once, she'd signed him up for baseball and soccer and karate. But Eddie only learned that he wasn't very good at hitting or kicking. Plus, there was never very much talking involved. So Eddie had found friends in books. Nathaniel Olmstead's stories were so vivid and strange, it was as if they had been plucked directly from Eddie's own brain. Maybe here, he thought, people would understand what that felt like.

He locked his bike to the stand and made his way up the stairs. When he pulled hard on the heavy glass door, the scent of old books wafted out. Eddie took a deep breath and stepped inside.

In the center of the main room, two shallow balconies stretched from wall to wall, fenced in by intricate wrought-iron railings. Tall shelves lined up vertically like teeth, running along the entire length of each floor. The books were a sight to behold—their spines were a jumbled mishmash of different sizes and colors. Some were new, but most were dusty, musty, and worn. Spiral staircases wound their way up through each floor. Though much of the room was cast in shadow, a skylight allowed the sun to spill down to the main level where Eddie stood. He gaped up at the beauty of the place and didn't realize his mouth was open until he heard a voice ask, "Can I help you?"

The librarian sat behind a large wooden desk. A nameplate on top of the desk said MRS. SINGH, ASSOCIATE LIBRARIAN. Her hair was wavy and dark, and her happy face was round. She smiled at Eddie, so he smiled back. Sometimes, book people were easier to talk to.

"Hi," he said. "I'm looking for a book about solving puzzles."

"Crossword puzzles?" she asked.

"No. Puzzles written in code."

"What kind of code?"

Eddie thought about that. "Like . . . this," he said, reaching into his bag and pulling out the book his mother had found the night before. He opened it to the middle and handed the book to her.

The librarian flipped through the pages. When she happened upon the first page, she glanced at him, squinting with what looked like concern. "Where did you get this?" said Mrs. Singh quietly.

"My mom gave it to me," said Eddie, suddenly unsure of himself. "Do you know what it means?"

The librarian's face turned red. "Of course I *don't* know what it means," she said, too forcefully. "Why would *I* know what it means?"

"I just thought . . . ," he said. He cleared his throat, trying to compose himself. Maybe it wasn't so easy to talk to book people, after all. "Can you recommend a book that might help?"

"No, actually," she said suddenly. "I'm quite busy, and the library closes at noon today." She turned her back on him and started typing something at the computer on the table behind her.

Eddie's face burned. Her attitude toward him had changed when she saw the first page. He wondered if the symbol written there had upset her? Or had it been Nathaniel Olmstead's name that sparked her irritation? Eddie decided not to ask. Instead, he quietly made his way to a cluster of computers near the back spiral staircase.

Pulling up the library's online catalog, Eddie suddenly had an idea. Since his own Nathaniel Olmstead books were packed away, it might be worth checking out a few from here—just to acquaint (or reacquaint) himself with some of the town's locations.

When he typed the author's name, a message appeared: *WE DID NOT FIND RESULTS FOR "NATHANIEL OLMSTEAD."* Confused, Eddie checked his spelling and entered the name again. But he received the same message. No results? How could that be? He glanced at the librarian at the front desk.

She was watching him.

When she saw him looking at her, she flinched and turned back to her computer. Eddie shivered. The librarian must not be a fan of Nathaniel Olmstead.

Eddie understood that some people didn't think Olmstead's books were very good, that they weren't considered literature. Still, it seemed odd that the man's hometown library wouldn't carry his own books, even if there was supposed to be an—

Olmstead Curse . . .

The tow truck driver's words echoed in Eddie's head. He closed his eyes and took a deep breath. Don't be silly, he told himself. It's only a story, right?

After searching the catalog for books about codes, Eddie climbed the stairs to the second floor and wandered into a row of shelves hidden in shadow. Even in the dim light, he managed to find *The History of Cryptography*. At least this should get me started, he thought.

Eddie headed back downstairs and reluctantly approached the front desk, where Mrs. Singh pretended to ignore him. After a few seconds, he said, "I'd like to check out this book, please."

Finally, she turned around with a huff and a sigh. "Your library card?" she said, holding out her hand to him. She waved her fingers impatiently.

"I . . . don't have one."

"Mmm-hmm," said Mrs. Singh. Eddie almost expected her to tell him that they were not issuing any new cards, but she reached under her desk, pulled out a piece of paper and a pencil, and handed them to him. Without looking at him, she said, "Fill this out." Eddie wrote down his new address and phone number and handed the paper back to Mrs. Singh.

"You're new in town?" she said curiously. Eddie merely nodded. As she turned around, she began to chew on her lip.

While he waited for her to process his new card, he flipped through the heavy book. It was filled with all sorts of confusing language—almost as weird as that of *The Enigmatic Manuscript*. Strange words like *cipher, algorithm, scytale, skipjack,* and *cryptanalysis* jumped off the page. There was so much *stuff* shoved between the covers, he wasn't even sure if he would be able to understand everything.

"Here you go," said Mrs. Singh. She handed him a small

peach-colored paper card on which was printed *Gatesweed Public Library, a place where stories are told.*

"Thank you," he said, as politely as possible. Eddie shoved the book in his bag, hiked it onto his shoulders, and struggled to open the library door.

Once outside, Eddie could not deny that it was a lovely day. Puffy clouds hovered over the hills, and a warm breeze skirted around the corner of the library. When Eddie unlocked his bike, he decided to ride over to the park and flip through his new library book. He crossed Center Street and followed the path through the middle of the town green. Like the rest of the town, the park was strangely deserted. There were several benches planted randomly in the grass. Eddie hopped off his bike and was about to find a place to sit when he heard an odd whispering sound from across the lawn.

The sound came from the direction of a bronze bust perched on top of a rectangular marble pedestal. The gray slab stood in the center of an old granite circle. Dandelions filled wide spaces where the slate had cracked over time. A plaque was attached to the front of the pedestal, but from where he stood, Eddie couldn't read what it said. He rested his bike on the sidewalk and trampled across the tall grass.

When he got closer, Eddie could see that the face of the bust had been destroyed, as if by a large blunt instrument. The nose had been mashed flat. Where its eyes should have been were two dark holes. Its lips were mangled into a permanent gaping howl. As he got even closer, the whispering sound grew louder.

Whist-whist-whist-whist-whist-whist.

It almost seemed as though the head was trying to speak to him through its distorted mouth. Eddie's hands went numb. He clutched the straps of his book bag against his shoulders. The pungent smell of bleach filled the air. How strange, he thought. Then, from the edge of the stone circle, he realized he could finally read the plaque: DEXTER AUGUST, 1717–1779.

Sam had mentioned this place. Eddie had actually found one of Olmstead's inspirations! Nathaniel Olmstead had written about the bust of Dexter August in *The Ghost in the Poet's Mansion.* It wasn't quite how Eddie had pictured it when he'd read the book; in Nathaniel Olmstead's version, Mr. August's face had not been vandalized.

The sound of something splashing came from the other side of the statue, startling Eddie. He stumbled off the edge of the granite circle.

A second later, he noticed a face peering at him from around the marble base. Before he could see it clearly, the face disappeared and the whispering sound began again. "Hello?" he said, trying to keep his voice from shaking. Keeping his distance from the bust, Eddie made his way to the other side.

A skinny man dressed in a wrinkly blue uniform knelt in the center of the granite circle. He scrubbed at the marble pedestal with a heavy wood brush. *Whist-whist-whist-whist-whist-whist.* Beside him sat a squat red metal bucket. After a moment, Eddie realized the man was the same police officer who had abandoned his family on Black Ribbon Road yesterday.

Eddie could hear the man muttering when he noticed what the police officer was scrubbing at. Someone had sprayed black paint in the primitive shape of a face onto the back of the pedestal. Two black squiggles for eyes dripped down the stone where the paint had been sprayed on thick. Below the eyes, one blunt, almost straight line grinned grimly. On the ground, behind where the police officer knelt, Eddie noticed more graffiti, huge words painted directly onto the broken granite. *THE WOMAN IS WATCHING.*

Eddie hiked his bag higher onto his shoulder. The woman is watching? What woman? Who is she watching? He glanced at the library, where the glass doors stared at him darkly. He wondered if Mrs. Singh was watching him from behind her desk.

Finally, the man looked at him, holding up his hand to block the sun's glare. He scowled. "It's not coming off this time."

This time? Had someone done this before? Eddie wondered. "I'm sorry," he said, feeling for some reason as if the officer blamed him.

"Oh, it's you," said the man, suddenly recognizing him. Eddie expected him to finish with *You made it home all right,* or *Sorry I couldn't be of more help yesterday,* or at the very least, *You lived!*

But the man simply stared at him expectantly, as if he anticipated Eddie to sprout wings and fly away.

The man's silence made him feel weird. "I, uh . . . I'll let you get back to work," Eddie said, stepping into the grass, heading toward his bike. The police officer continued to stare at him as he walked away. Eventually, the whispering sound began again as the man went back to scrubbing at the black paint. *Whist-whist-whist.*

Eddie began to run. When he reached the sidewalk where his bike lay, he noticed something painted onto the window of a store on the other side of the park.

BOOKS.

This time, the paint was not graffiti.

Even though he was sort of freaked out, Eddie couldn't resist. His mother had mentioned a bookstore in Gatesweed. This must be it. A bookstore was always cozier than a library—more comforting—a familiar place in an unfamiliar town. He picked up his bike from the sidewalk. Keeping far away from the weird cop, he walked his bike across the grass and crossed the street.

The bookstore was in the lower portion of a two-story white wooden house, the last in a row of buildings that curved along the park. A green-and-white-striped awning reached out toward Eddie, shading the house's porch from the sunlight. Glancing over his shoulder toward the park, Eddie noticed the cop staring but decided to ignore him.

He crept up the stairs and pressed his nose to the window of the store, holding up his hands to block out the glare. Dim lights hung from the ceiling, and bookshelves stretched up so high that tall ladders leaned against them in several spots. The store looked empty.

"We're not open," said a voice behind him.

Eddie spun around to see a blond-haired boy who'd spent too much of the summer exposed to the sun. The skin on the boy's nose was peeling. Eddie thought he smelled like insect repellent. Eddie stood there with his mouth open, barely able to breathe. Why was it that he could approach an adult librarian without a problem, but when facing the possibility of conversation with someone his own age, Eddie's brain shut tight?

"What do you want?" said the boy.

"Nuh," said Eddie, turning sunburn red. He'd meant to say *Nothing*, but was only able to spit out the first part of the word.

The boy examined Eddie quizzically before reaching around and opening the door. Cool air breezed out. Eddie was about to ask what time he should come back when the boy brushed past Eddie, closed the door, and locked it.

Embarrassed, Eddie almost turned to leave when the window display caught his attention. He came closer to the glass to make sure his eyes weren't fooling him.

Sitting on the table near the window ledge was a small display of Nathaniel Olmstead's books. A hand-painted sign propped up on the table read GATESWEED'S VERY OWN. The books were stacked precisely in several piles. *The Ghost in the Poet's Mansion. The Revenge of the Nightmarys. The Cat, the Quill, and the Candle. The Wrath of the Wendigo.* They were all there; however, these were not the books that caught Eddie's attention.

At the far edge of the table sat a small stack of leather-bound books that had a different title.

The Enigmatic Manuscript.

Eddie dropped his book bag onto the porch. Bending over, he opened the bag's front pocket and pulled out the book his mother had found the night before. Holding it up, Eddie compared it to the books sitting on the table. They seemed to be exactly the same. Would the inside of the books be the same too? Eddie felt his heart pumping. He could see the blond boy moving around near the back of the store. Eddie took a deep breath, realizing what he must do. The characters in Nathaniel Olmstead's books never solved any of their mysteries without taking a risk or two.

Before he could think to stop himself, Eddie knocked on the window. When the blond boy peered around the corner of a bookshelf, Eddie waved and forced himself to smile.

"We're closed!" shouted the boy before ducking away. His words hit Eddie in the chest like a fast, hard baseball. This wasn't going to be easy. Maybe he should leave. But no, he told himself. *Ronald Plimpton* would not have given up so easily.

He raised his hand again and continued to knock. He didn't stop until the blond boy had come all the way to the front of the store. Angrily, the boy shouted through the door, "What is wrong with you?"

"I—I wanted to ask you something," Eddie stammered.

"Yeah . . . ?" said the boy, looking as if he were about to walk away. His voice sounded muffled through the glass.

"I wanted to know about that book on the table in the window. *The Enigmatic Manuscript.*"

"What about it?"

"I was wondering if you knew when Nathaniel Olmstead wrote it?"

The boy made a face like Eddie was crazy. "Wrote it?"

"Yeah," said Eddie. "What year did the book come out?"

"Nathaniel Olmstead didn't write a book called *The Enigmatic Manuscript.* Nobody wrote *The Enigmatic Manuscript.*"

Eddie shook his head, confused. The blond boy rolled his eyes, grabbed one of the books off the pile of *Enigmatic Manuscripts*, and opened it to a page in the middle. He held the book up to the window for Eddie to see.

"Blank," said the boy.

Eddie still didn't understand.

"The Enigmatic Manuscript is the name of my mother's store!" said the boy.

"The name of your mother's store?" said Eddie. He looked over his shoulder. The store's hanging placard sign stuck out from the pole at the top of the stairs, but it hung perpendicular to the street, so it was really only visible from either side of the stairs.

"We sell souvenir blank notebooks," the boy continued. "If you wanna buy one . . ." The boy spun around and started back toward the bookshelves. Over his shoulder, he called, "Then come back some other time."

"Wait!" cried Eddie, knocking on the window. When the boy turned around, Eddie quickly pressed the cover of his own copy of the book up to the window. "I don't want to buy one," he called through the glass. "I've already got one. And I think it might have belonged to Nathaniel Olmstead."

The boy paused for a few moments before returning to the front of the store again. He unlocked the door, opened it, and stood in the doorway. "Why do you think that?" he asked.

Suddenly, Eddie felt foolish. "Because mine's not blank." He awkwardly held out the book.

The boy took it from Eddie and brushed the cover with his fingers. It was obviously older than the ones in the store. He turned it over and examined the spine. When he opened the cover and saw the first page, his eyes widened. A moment later, he squinted skeptically. "Where'd you get this?" His reaction reminded Eddie of the librarian's.

"My parents bought it at an antiques fair just north of here," said Eddie. "But look." He reached forward to turn the page.

"Whoa," said the boy, examining the strange words. "What is this?"

"That's what I'm trying to figure out," said Eddie. "In his books, Nathaniel Olmstead always uses codes and stuff. Looks like he went a little bit overboard with this one."

"Right, I know. I've got all of his books upstairs in my bedroom."

"You do?" Eddie was surprised. He had begun to think no one in Gatesweed appreciated Nathaniel Olmstead like he did. "Maybe you can tell me how Nathaniel Olmstead ended up with a souvenir book from your mom's store?"

"Duh . . . Nathaniel Olmstead lived in Gatesweed. My mom knew him."

Eddie was speechless. Forgetting the mystery for the moment, he wondered if Nathaniel Olmstead might have stood in this very spot.

"A long time ago, my mom told me Nathaniel Olmstead was the one who suggested she open the store. He even came up with the name."

"That is so cool. Did you know him?"

"No way," said the boy. "I was, like, zero years old when he disappeared. Thirteen years ago, on Halloween, he was supposed to give a reading at my mom's store, but he never showed up. She tried calling him for the next few weeks . . . but she's never heard from him again. No one has."

"Huh," said Eddie. "That's so weird." Then he had an idea. "Hey, what do you know about the Olmstead Curse?"

The boy gave him a sharp look. He pressed his lips together, then glanced over Eddie's shoulder toward the park. When Eddie turned around, he saw the police officer near the bronze bust glaring at them.

"I—I gotta go," said the boy suddenly.

"But—"

"I'm sorry. I'm not supposed to . . ." The boy shoved the book into Eddie's hands. He turned around and closed the door to the bookstore, leaving Eddie alone on the porch.

Across the street, the police officer tossed his brush into the bucket with a splash.

Eddie decided to ride his bike back home. After hearing Sam mention the possibility of an Olmstead Curse yesterday, he had expected that he might encounter some weird things in Gatesweed. After all, Olmstead stories were pretty weird, so it made sense that the place where he wrote them might be weird too. But after his experience that morning, he thought he could use a break from *weird* for a few hours. Besides, the cryptology book was too heavy to simply carry around while he searched for more sites from Olmstead's books.

When he opened his bedroom door, Eddie found his mother sitting on his bed, facing the window with her back to him. "Mom?" Eddie said. She yelped, leapt off his bed, and spun around. When she saw that it was Eddie, relief flooded her face.

"Edgar, you scared me so badly I nearly flew out the window!"

"What are you doing?" Eddie asked, curious. Then he noticed what she was holding in her hand, his copy of *The Wrath of the Wendigo.*

She held up the book and said, "Guilty as charged. I was flipping through your book. I'm sorry I barged in here, but when I was unpacking this morning, I found a box that belongs to you." The small cardboard box sat at the end of his bed. "Since you were looking for these books last night, I brought them up."

"Thanks," said Eddie.

"Can I borrow this one?" she said, blushing. "I know it's creepy fantasy stuff, which isn't usually my thing. . . ." She hestitated. "It's sort of silly, but . . ." She flipped open the back cover and showed Eddie the picture of Nathaniel Olmstead. "I had a feeling that I should look him up. I thought maybe since we live in his old town now, he could help me." She paused, then said, "It's been so difficult lately, I'm not even sure I *should* be a writer anymore."

"Of course you should be a writer," said Eddie. "You love writing."

"But I'm beginning to think I'm not any good!" said Mom. "I read you that *epic* poem I wrote last week. It was ridiculous!" She threw her arms wide and said in a deep, dramatic voice, *"How woebegone was Constance Meade? She had one glass eye and couldn't read!* What was I thinking? I don't even know what I *want* to write anymore. Forget this rhyming stuff. . . . I've got to find a great *story* to tell."

Eddie walked across the room to his bed, sat down on his mattress, and took off his sneakers. "New town, new stories. Isn't that what Dad said?"

"He did say that, didn't he? The funny thing is . . . I think I might actually have an idea for a new story," said Mom. "Thanks for letting me borrow this." She waved the book. "Let's hope this Nathaniel Olmstead person knows what he's doing."

"He knows," Eddie said. "I'm sure of it."

Mom went back downstairs. After unpacking some more boxes, Eddie spent some time hunched over his desk scanning the mysterious book, searching for a clue. After staring at the page, the letters all started to blend together, and he couldn't concentrate.

To clear his head, Eddie hauled the library book out of his bag. He went through it slowly, trying to understand the confusing academic writing, but ultimately, the book wasn't much help. For a while, there didn't seem to be anything in it that resembled the code in *The Enigmatic Manuscript.*

Finally, in a chapter called "The Science of the Secret Message," he came across a symbol similar to the one written on the first page of the book. The symbol was called pi. Memories of Mrs. Benson's math class came back to Eddie. He already knew pi was a Greek letter that stood for 3.14; still, he tried to read more about it. The letter represented a constant relationship between the circumference and diameter of a circle. But he didn't see what that had to do with anything.

Just before dinner, Eddie's father finally managed to set up the Internet connection. Thinking about what the tow truck driver had said, Eddie searched for a link between the names "Jeremy" and "Gatesweed." Near the top of the page, he found what he was looking for: a headline for an archived article in a journal called *The Black Hood Herald.* The article described an investigation, which had occurred almost twenty years earlier, into the disappearance of a twelve-year-old boy from his bedroom one October night. His name had been Jeremy Quakerly.

This must be the boy Sam had been talking about, Eddie thought. His childhood friend had disappeared. How horrible . . . But what did this have to do with the supposed Olmstead Curse? The article didn't mention anything about curses.

Next, Eddie searched for the words "Olmstead Curse." He received several results, but one paragraph leapt clearly off the screen. It was from a Web site called Cassandra's Calendar, posted several years ago.

Some citizens of Gatesweed are calling these incidents the unfortunate consequence of the aptly named "Olmstead Curse." Local superstition says the author's stories have wreaked havoc on the town itself. As strange as it may seem, many blame the missing author himself for the recent closing of the Black Ribbon Mill. Representatives for Mr. Olmstead pass off such comments as unsubstantiated hogwash. Outside of Gatesweed, such hogwash continues to work wonders for the author's sales. . . .

Weird, thought Eddie. He read through several more search results. From the articles, Eddie gathered that, for some reason, people in Gatesweed believed Nathaniel Olmstead's stories were dangerous. Eddie didn't understand.

How could words be dangerous?

More important, Eddie still wasn't sure if there was a connection between the supposed curse and the book his mother had found in the barn. Certainly, the biggest clue of the day had been the bookstore. Now at least Eddie knew where the book had come from. He wondered if the blond boy who smelled like bug spray would be at school tomorrow. It was possible that they might even be in the same classes. If he could get up the nerve, Eddie would have another chance to ask for his help. As he went downstairs for dinner, he decided that's what he would do.

5

The first day of school, Eddie kept embarrassing himself.

During homeroom, Ms. Phelps made him introduce himself. As he'd already learned, new kids were rare to Gatesweed. Everyone already seemed to know each other. Eddie was so nervous and spoke so quietly, Ms. Phelps forced him to repeat everything he said. Twice! His face burned when his new classmates rolled their eyes at him.

In the cafeteria line, Eddie meant to ask the lunch lady for a tuna melt, but he stammered when he ordered and accidentally called it a *tuba* melt. Everyone behind him started laughing; one boy made farting noises.

Finally, after lunch, he bumped into a girl, knocking her book bag off her shoulder. He'd been thinking about the code and didn't see her coming around the corner. "I'm so sorry!" said Eddie, helping pick up the bag. He half expected her to start complaining, but instead she barely looked at him.

"It's fine. I can get it," said the girl.

She wore a faded black T-shirt, worn-out black jeans, and boots that looked as if they'd been boiled. Her stringy hair hung down either side of her face, tucked behind her big ears. Her skin was pale, but her eyes were dark circles. She looked like a character he imagined would live in a Nathaniel Olmstead book. He realized he was staring, and he felt his face turning red. But before he could introduce himself, the girl blinked at him, fixed her bag, and walked briskly away.

"Nice one," said someone from across the hallway.

When Eddie turned, he saw the blond boy from the bookstore standing near Eddie's locker with his arms folded across his chest. He wore a navy blue polo shirt and dark jeans; he no longer smelled like bug spray. Eddie felt his stomach clench. Last night, he'd imagined that the boy would be here at school, but after yesterday, Eddie thought he would have to track him down to ask for his help. Now he felt unprepared.

"You might want to stay away from her," said the boy.

"Who—who is she?" said Eddie as he put away the textbooks he'd been given that morning.

"Freaky Maggie Ringer. She lives up near the Olmstead estate."

Eddie blushed. "Why do you think she's a freak?"

"Look at her."

"Because she dresses in black?"

"Well . . . yeah. And she doesn't have any friends."

Eddie knew what that felt like. "That doesn't mean she's a freak."

"If you say so," said the boy. He tugged at his belt loop anxiously. After a moment, he said, "I'm Harris. Harris May. From the bookstore yesterday?"

"Uh, yeah, I remember you," said Eddie. "I'm Eddie."

"Why didn't you tell me you lived here?" said Harris. "In Gatesweed," he added.

"I didn't really have time," said Eddie. "You sorta took off."

Harris blushed. "Yeah. Sorry about that. I never saw you before. Everyone knows everyone else in this town, but sometimes weird people pass through. . . . I thought you were—"

"One of them?" said Eddie. "Gee, thanks."

Harris laughed. "I didn't mean it like that. It's just . . . Wally was watching you."

"Wally?" said Eddie.

"The one cop this town can afford to keep on its force," said Harris. "He doesn't like Olmstead hunters."

"Olmstead hunters?"

"Fans. They're my mom's biggest customers. Nobody else ever really comes to Gatesweed. When you mentioned the Olmstead Curse stuff . . ." He sighed. "Wally had stopped by in the morning, before you showed up. He spent, like, an hour interrogating me about the new graffiti in the park. He thinks *I* had something to do with it."

"Did you?"

Harris smirked. "No," he said simply. "It's actually really annoying. Every few months something else appears. Wally usually blames me."

" 'The Woman Is Watching' . . . Does the graffiti have something to do with the Olmstead . . . *Curse*?" Since Harris just mentioned the word, Eddie figured it was okay to say it now too.

"That's sort of hard to explain . . . and the bell's about to ring," Harris said, glancing down the hallway. "Which way are you walking?"

Eddie shrugged. "Not sure. Mr. Weir's English class?"

Harris nodded. "This way. Come on."

Eddie closed his locker and spun the combination. His heart raced, partly because he thought he might start finding answers to his Olmstead questions, but also because Harris actually seemed pretty nice. He didn't want to screw things up by saying something stupid like "tuba melt" again.

Leading them down the hallway, Harris continued, "So you *really* don't know anything about the stuff written in that book you showed me?"

"No," said Eddie. "Other than the fact that it's some sort of code I can't figure out by myself. I showed it to the librarian in town yesterday. She started acting really weird."

"What did she do?" said Harris, surprised.

"She said she couldn't help me," said Eddie.

"Did you show it to anybody else?"

"Only my parents. They're the ones who gave it to me," said Eddie. "Do *you* know anything about the code?"

Harris shook his head. "Not the *code* . . ." He paused for a few seconds, then quickly and quietly said, "You have to promise not to tell anyone I said anything. It's really important, because I could get in a lot of trouble. . . . Some people in town don't like that my mom still sells Olmstead books. They'd rather just forget Nathaniel Olmstead ever existed. Stupid. Sort of hard when his books are, like, everywhere. There's been talk about shutting down the bookstore. Wally's looking for any excuse."

Eddie didn't hesitate before answering, "I won't say anything to anyone about anything." The hallways were starting to empty. He noticed the room number he was looking for on the door to his right.

"You don't have anything to do after school today, do you?" said Harris.

"Not yet."

"Good." Harris smiled. "I hope you rode here on that bike I saw you riding yesterday. You're going to need it."

6

After the last bell, Eddie called his mother and told her he was hanging out with a friend, then the two boys rode their bikes up into the Gatesweed Hills. Black Ribbon Road carved a twisted path through their dark valleys. They headed in the direction from which his family had come on moving day. Eddie wasn't sure where Harris was taking him, but at this point it almost didn't matter—he was having fun. In Heaverhill, the roads had never zigzagged like this, and the kids had never asked him to come along.

While they rode, Harris told Eddie about growing up in Gatesweed. He explained that most of their classmates lived on the outskirts of town, out in the farm country. He and his mother had never lived anywhere other than here, and he couldn't really imagine what it would be like to leave. Eddie told Harris about the car accident, leaving out the part when he'd thought the animal was a monster. He didn't want to sound like a freak. He mentioned the weird people he'd seen in Gatesweed so far—the policeman, the tow truck guy, the librarian. Harris nodded, as if he knew exactly what Eddie was talking about. He agreed that some people in the town could be a little paranoid and protective of each other in a way.

They rode in silence for a while before Harris brought up Nathaniel Olmstead's books. They'd both read all of them at least twice. Harris told him that his favorite one was *The Ghost in the Poet's Mansion.* He really loved the part about the secret passage behind the kitchen cabinet that led to the magical library. Eddie told him that his favorite book was *The Rumor of the Haunted Nunnery.* The way Ronald Plimpton solved all the riddles was so exciting. Harris disagreed that Ronald was an expert. He insisted that Ronald had gotten all of the most helpful information from his grandfather.

Eddie noticed that Harris was a little sensitive about who liked the books better, so he made sure not to argue about it. Eddie didn't want to blow a potential friendship, so he changed the topic to Nathaniel Olmstead himself. He asked Harris what he thought might really have happened to him.

"I'm not sure. Some people say he got in some sort of trouble and decided to hide for a while."

"From who? The librarian?"

"Yeah . . . right!" Harris stopped and stood on his bike in the road.

On the right was the tall rusty iron fence the tow truck had driven by on Saturday. It was set back in the woods about thirty yards from the road, stretching about a hundred feet in both directions. Farther ahead was a small gate. Someone had chained it shut. Nathaniel Olmstead's house sat on the grassy clearing at the top of the hill. The boys stood at the base of the overgrown driveway. Beyond the gate, the road curved around the steep slope and disappeared into the trees. Gnarled vines hung from the branches, and brown grass grew in patches out of the pebbly dirt.

At the gate, Eddie was certain they would not be able to go any farther. But Harris got off his bike, hiked into the brush, pushed aside some of the thick vines, and revealed a gap wide enough for them to squeeze through one at a time.

"We're going in?" asked Eddie, suddenly remembering the animal his father had hit only two days earlier. "Is it safe?"

"Hmm," said Harris. "Probably not. But I can't show you what you need to see if we don't. Come on, we'll leave our bikes here."

"Won't someone see them?" All of a sudden, Eddie felt nervous. The faces of the people he'd met in Gatesweed scowled at him when he closed his eyes. "We'll get in trouble."

"Lay it down flat. You can't see them from the road. Believe me, I've checked."

"Then you've been here before?" Eddie asked.

Harris rested his bike behind a small evergreen bush. "What do you think?" he said.

Eddie shrugged, laid his bike next to Harris's, then followed him through the broken gate. Together, they hiked the rest of the way up the long driveway.

At the top of the hill, the house sat in silence. Eddie couldn't believe he was actually here, seeing the view Nathaniel Olmstead had seen every day. He turned around to take in the countryside. He wanted to see where the house stood. Farther up Black Ribbon Road was the spot where they'd stopped on Saturday. In the opposite direction were the hills through which the road dipped and curved. The town of Gatesweed lay beyond the small, smooth peaks. The blue sky made the house even creepier, as if on a day such as this, the house should have been alive and lived in. But covered in vines and falling apart, the house almost seemed to whisper, *Welcome . . .*

"What's the matter?" Harris said.

"Nothing. Why?"

"You look . . . I don't know . . . weird or something."

"Sorry," said Eddie, stepping toward the house. Eddie pulled a clingy nettle off his sleeve. Goose bumps raced across his skin. He crossed his arms and shuddered. Those dark upstairs windows were dead eyes, but they watched nonetheless. "I don't know. It's creepier up here than I thought it would be."

"This is nothing," said Harris, raising an eyebrow.

The sound of crickets and chirping birds was interrupted

only by the wind and Eddie's imagination. Harris led him to the back of the house, where a small pasture stretched down the other side of the hill. About three hundred feet away, five rows of small trees dared the boys to come closer.

"An orchard," said Harris. "I don't think the fruit grows here anymore." Beyond the orchard another hill arched up. A thick blanket of trees covered a small ridge. "And there"—

Harris pointed—"is the Nameless Woods."

"Why doesn't it have a name?" asked Eddie.

"That *is* its name." Harris trotted off down the hill and across the pasture. He called over his shoulder to Eddie, who stood frozen like a statue. "And that's where we're going."

Once over the small ridge, they came to a green carpet of plants stretching under a flat expanse of trees. They continued their hike in silence. Under the dense canopy of leaves, the light filtered dimly, almost green. The forest was surprisingly dark. The smaller trees twisted toward the rare rays of sunlight. Fighting for space in the rocky soil, some of the bigger tree roots bulged like the swollen tentacles of deep-ocean creatures. As Harris led Eddie into the woods, they waded through a shallow sea of ankle-high plants. There was no path, only dead leaves and prickly brush. Eddie hoped he didn't end up with poison ivy.

Finally, they reached a place where the trees did not obscure the sky. A circular clearing stretched out in front of them. It was approximately twenty feet in diameter. No greenery grew here. The ground was covered with small rocks. Dust hung in the air.

From the edge of the clearing, Eddie could see a white figure standing just off the center of the circle, closer to the other side. It looked like a ghost.

"What is that?" Eddie whispered.

"A statue," Harris whispered back. "Come on."

They slowly made their way across the clearing. A raven heckled them from a nearby tree, but Eddie couldn't take his eyes off the figure. Standing in front of her, he could make out more details. The statue was gleaming white—a girl about his own height. She wore a simple robe that bunched at her shoulders, draped at the waist, and fell, pleated all the way to her feet, like something out of a painting he'd seen in an art history book. Her hair was draped in simple wavy ringlets past her shoulders. Her arms were bare and her toes peeked out from the bottom of the robe. The small-domed base on which she stood was carved with all sorts of beasts, dragons, sphinxes, and other strange creatures Eddie did not recognize. Her smile was almost undetectable as her milky eyes stared at Eddie and sent chills up his spine. Her arms were extended, and in her hands she held an open book tilted toward herself.

"What does the book say?" said Eddie.

"See for yourself," said Harris, staying back.

Feeling almost nauseated, Eddie stepped forward, stood on his toes, and peered over the edge of the stone pages.

"It's blank." Feeling a little too close to her gaze, Eddie stepped away from the statue. "She sort of looks familiar. . . ."

Harris smiled, raising an eyebrow. Eddie felt like he was missing something. Then it hit him.

"Isn't she from . . . ?"

"The Haunted Nunnery," said Harris. "Yup."

"Whoa," Eddie whispered. He'd found another of Nathaniel's inspirations. Up close, it looked exactly as he'd imagined.

Something small crunched through the brush outside of the clearing, and the raven cawed again. The noises made Eddie's skin prickle, but he told himself that these woods were filled with squirrels, chipmunks, and mice, all harmless creatures that were very good at making crunching sounds. Trying not to sound as freaked out as he felt, he nonchalantly asked, "This is cool and everything, but what does a statue have to do with my book?"

"I didn't bring you here to look at *a* statue. I brought you here to look at *this* statue. And I don't think you've looked close enough."

"What do you mean?"

Harris crept close to the statue and leaned underneath her book. "Here."

Eddie ducked under the book too. There was something

carved there. Eddie leaned closer to see what it was. The symbol from the first page of *The Enigmatic Manuscript* was engraved clearly into the book's stone cover.

A cool rush crept underneath Eddie's clothes, tickling his skin. "What the heck is going on here?" he said.

Harris didn't say anything for a moment. He stood next to Eddie and stared at him. Finally, he said, "Creepy, huh? I know the feeling."

Eddie reached out and ran his finger along the cold stone spine of the book. "How did you hear about this place?"

"After Nathaniel Olmstead disappeared," said Harris, "the town sent out a search party. They came across this clearing. It's sort of become a local legend in Gatesweed. Nobody knows for sure who this statue is supposed to be, who carved it, or why it's here."

"Really?" said Eddie. "Hasn't anyone even tried to guess?"

"I've heard some of the high school students say it's a gravestone," Harris said, shoving his hands into his pants pockets.

"A gravestone out here in the middle of the woods?" The thought gave Eddie goose bumps again. "Who does it belong to?"

Harris shook his head. "No one knows. There's no name on the stone," he whispered. "But they also say . . . its ghost haunts these woods."

"A ghost?" said Eddie, glancing over his shoulder. "What kind of ghost?"

"Some people say they've seen the ghost of an old woman wandering around Nathaniel Olmstead's estate."

"Really?" said Eddie. He looked up at the statue. She stared at him blankly.

"That's not the only thing people have seen up here," said Harris. "People tell stories of strange animals. Weird noises. Stuff like that."

Strange animals? Eddie's stomach squelched. "The thing that totaled my dad's car on Black Ribbon Road was pretty weird looking," he said. He still didn't mention that he'd thought it was a monster. The accident had happened so fast, he wasn't sure what he'd seen anymore. "Did you see anything strange the last time you came up here?"

Harris laughed. "If I had, do you think I'd be wandering around in these woods with you?"

Eddie chuckled too. "I guess not."

"I mean, yeah, I heard some noises I couldn't explain," said Harris. "And once or twice I thought I saw a shadow move, but when I turned to look, nothing was there. Then again, I'm pretty skeptical when it comes to stuff like this. Sure, I like Olmstead's books, but I know the difference between what's real and what's made up." Eddie didn't quite believe him. Harris continued, "People in town are pretty serious about the legend of the statue, though. They talk. Some people think that if you stay up here too long, the ghost of the woman will follow you home. She'll haunt you until you go crazy. That's probably why the librarian freaked out when you showed her your book. Mrs. Singh's definitely heard about the statue's symbol. When she saw it on the first page of your book, she must have thought you'd already been up here. She didn't want the ghost to follow her too."

"That's dumb," said Eddie, forcing a laugh. "People in Gatesweed really believe that?"

Harris scoffed. "Yeah, actually. Some of them really do. But then again, a few of them *are* crazy, if you ask me."

"Seems like *someone's* crazy enough to graffiti that statue in town." When Harris gave him a knowing look, Eddie continued, "So weird. Someone had painted this awful face onto the pedestal, with swirling black squiggles for eyes."

Harris smiled reluctantly and crossed his arms. "Once, someone spray-painted it on the side of my mother's store," he said. "*The Woman Is Watching.* In big black letters. It took forever to clean it off."

"Someone graffitied your store because of the Olmstead Curse?" Eddie asked. "They don't want her selling his books?"

"Exactly." Harris nodded. "They think the less people who come through town, the less . . . trouble there will be here. To them, Gatesweed is filled with dirty little secrets, Nathaniel Olmstead's disappearance being number one. But my mother was friends with him. And she'll never stop selling his books in her store—no matter how many times people paint nasty things on her front porch . . . or how many people believe his monsters are real."

The pair of red-rimmed yellow eyes blinked in Eddie's memory. He remembered the articles he'd read on the Internet about the curse. "People *really* think his monsters are real?" he said, clutching his book bag even tighter.

"Yeah," said Harris. "Some people do. Like the animals people say they've seen in these woods. I've never seem them, but I've heard people say they look like the ones Nathaniel writes about. Everything that happens in this town gets blamed on him—and he's not even here anymore. People stopped going to the movie theater on Main Street because of the things they said lived behind the screen. And the mills closed down after the owners kept finding huge gouges in their machinery. People said they looked like bite marks. And, of course, a small group of people blamed the New Mill Bridge collapse on Nathaniel's trolls. After everything else, that one was pretty much inevitable. Lots of people left town when the mills closed. That sort of destroyed Gatesweed, so it makes sense that people need someone to blame, but still . . ."

"What about the symbol on the statue?" said Eddie. "Do you know what that means? I read something about the Greek letter pi, which looks almost exactly like the symbol carved here." He pointed at the girl.

"Right . . . from math class," said Harris. "Maybe. We could look into it, but I'm not very good at that subject. And I don't know a thing about Greek. What I do know is that the book you found is important. I was so happy when I saw you in school today . . . that you weren't just an Olmstead hunter, chased away by old Wally the Weasel. That's what my mom calls him," said Harris, with a smirk. "I was thinking about your book all night. The code *has* to mean something. The symbol on the statue is the connection. I brought you here so that you'd understand. . . . The secret of the book in your bag isn't just about a code. It's about this place, this statue. It might be about Nathaniel Olmstead himself. Who knows . . . maybe if we solve it, we'll find out what really happened to him. Maybe we can clear his name. Then people will leave my mom alone."

"Yeah, totally!" said Eddie. "Nathaniel Olmstead would also probably give us his autograph or something . . . if he's, you know . . . still alive." As he said the words, he felt foolish, disrespectful—especially in this place, so close to where the man had lived. He wandered to the opposite side of the circle. "So you *do* think the book might have belonged to Nathaniel Olmstead?"

The land sloped down quickly. At the bottom where it leveled out, the hill was met by a lake, about thirty feet across. The trees on the other shore concealed a steep, rocky hillside that jutted high above the water. Through the thick foliage, the tree roots were visible clinging, almost clutching, at the cliffside. Near the water's edge, several long, leafy branches hung down from the trees and dangled just above the calm surface, tickling their own reflections with stringy shadows.

"If not, at least it belonged to someone who knows about the Nameless Woods, the Nameless Lake," said Harris, following Eddie across the clearing to the top of the slope, "and the symbol on the statue."

"Which could be anyone in town," said Eddie. "Right?" He picked up a pebble from the edge of the clearing before heading down the hill.

"Yeah," said Harris, "but no matter who it belonged to in the past, now it's up to us to figure it out."

Eddie nodded, excited. Was Harris suggesting they work together? That they become friends? "Yeah," he said as they neared the edge of the lake. "It's up to us."

"So how should we start?" said Harris.

At the shore, Eddie tossed the pebble. It bounced across the sky's reflection, splashing several times before disappearing underneath the surface. "I've already taken the one code book out of the library," said Eddie. "But it's really confusing and not much help." The raven called to them from the top of the hill near the statue, louder this time.

"Forget about it then," said Harris. "I'm sure we can find some sort of pattern on our own."

Eddie was about to take *The Enigmatic Manuscript* out of his bag so they could get started, when near the far shore, the calm surface of the water suddenly rippled, as if something large had risen from below. The raven at the top of the hill took off for the sky. Wide-eyed, the boys looked at each other.

"I think the sun's starting to go down," said Harris, stepping away from the shore.

"Did you see that?" said Eddie. Small waves disturbed the water at the center of the lake. Eddie stepped forward, trying to peer through the blue sky's opaque reflection. He could see a dark shape shifting and squirming in the hazy depths fifteen feet from the shore. The shape reminded Eddie of a fast-moving storm cloud, swirling and rolling in upon itself as it grew stronger. The forest behind him was suddenly quiet, as if all its inhabitants did not want to be heard. From where he stood, Eddie could see the dark cloudy shape rise to the surface of the water from below, creating a black spot nearly five feet in diameter. The edges of the black spot seemed to pulsate and roil, spreading its wide fingers out across the top of the lake like a fist slowly opening. "Is it an oil slick?" Eddie asked.

"I don't know *what* it is," said Harris, staring at the spot intently as it continued to grow. Now it had doubled in size. It floated in stark contrast to the sky's blue reflection, turning the water black as it spread outward.

"It's coming up from the bottom of the lake." Eddie leaned forward. "Like a geyser." He was frightened, yet at the same time, he was curious. "Or maybe not. I can't really tell." He'd never seen anything like this before. After Harris's spooky stories about the woods and the town, he felt compelled to run away, but he also wanted to stay to see what would happen as the black shape grew and grew. This almost seemed like something that would happen in a Nathaniel Olmstead book, but, of course, Eddie told himself, those stories were not real, in spite of what people believed.

Now the dark shape in the middle of the lake was as large as a small island, taking up almost all of the water's surface. The blue reflection from above had been replaced by darkness from below, as if someone had covered the sky with a blanket; yet, when Eddie looked up, he could see the sun still shining somewhere beyond the canopy of trees near the horizon. Even so, the afternoon light barely broke through the treetops. Then Eddie noticed something even weirder. In the water, there began to appear little white specks of light, which wavered as the surface rippled slightly. Eddie was reminded of a book he'd read about phosphorescent algae. He also remembered reading about a type of shrimp capable of producing a small amount of light, like a firefly. But these specks of light didn't look like algae or shrimp or fireflies. They appeared to be something else—something familiar that Eddie couldn't quite name.

"Are those . . . stars?" whispered Harris.

The darkness reached the shore, so that now, except for the specks of light, the entire lake had turned black. The water did not merely look dirty—but impenetrable and infinite. Eddie cautiously leaned forward even farther. "You're right," he said. "It almost looks like . . . a reflection of the night sky." He glanced up at the cirrus clouds wisping in the afternoon light, then shook his head, baffled. He bent down and picked up another pebble from the edge of the water. He was about to toss it in to see what would happen, when Harris grabbed his arm.

"Don't," said Harris. "Look."

The specks of white had turned red. Eddie realized they no longer looked like the reflection of stars from above. Now the lights were clearly floating just below the water, close enough for Eddie to reach out and touch. The sight was almost hypnotic. Eddie began to feel dizzy. Suddenly, he knew what would happen next. He'd read about it in one of Nathaniel Olmstead's books on Saturday night.

"Eddie, get away." Harris yanked him backward as something large in the middle of the lake splashed the dark water. Several waves came rolling slowly toward the shore. Unable to look away, Eddie felt his skin go prickly with goose bumps. His mouth felt as if it was filled with dust. His hands were numb. Harris continued to pull on his sleeve. When Eddie glanced at him, he could see fright welling up in Harris's eyes. His mouth had fallen open, and his skin had turned ashen. Seeing Harris afraid made Eddie twice as scared as before.

Harris swiftly shot his finger to his lips and nodded toward the hillside. Slowly backing away, the boys made it to the edge of the woods. Several pine branches poked into Eddie's back. He jumped. The splashing in the middle of the lake stopped. The small waves finally rose up and rolled onto the pebbly beach, breaking and washing the shore in slow, steady rhythm. The soft lapping of the water was the only sound Eddie could hear. Then, several feet from the edge of the lake, a shape churned the water—something rising from the shallows below the surface. A muffled howl resonated faintly from its direction. Eddie's mouth dropped open in horror as he saw what looked like a long black snout and a flash of several sharp white teeth.

The boys turned and ran as fast as they could, slipping and sliding up the slope in the mud and dirt. At the top of the hill, the statue watched silently as the boys ran through the clearing and into the woods. Eddie followed Harris, leaping over large roots and half-buried rocks that jutted out of the ground every few feet. In some places, the trees had grown densely together. Trying not to slip in patches of silt and leaves, the boys weaved back and forth as if through an obstacle course. Even though he was nearly out of breath, Eddie glanced over his shoulder.

But there was nothing there.

Still, he wanted to get away from this place as quickly as possible. Eddie sprinted into the woods, clutching the straps of his bag, which bounced against his back. At the edge of the flatland, the boys briefly caught their breath before heading over the ridge, through the orchard, past Nathaniel Olmstead's house, and all the way down the long driveway. By the time they got to their bikes, Eddie was feeling faint.

He dropped to the side of the road and hung his head between his knees. After he caught his breath, he glanced up at Harris, who was leaning against the fence in shock. "What the heck just happened?" said Eddie. "I thought I saw . . . dogs . . . coming out of the water for us!"

"I'm not sure what I saw," said Harris, red-faced and weary. "But I have an idea." He pushed himself away from the fence and stumbled toward his bike. "There's something else I think you should see."

"It's not another statue, is it?" said Eddie.

Harris shook his head, lifted the handlebar, and set his bicycle upright at the edge of the road. After swinging his leg over the seat, he kicked at Eddie's bike, which was still on its side in the brush. "Do you think you're okay enough to ride this thing back to my place?"

Eddie nodded.

"Because we should probably get the heck out of here."

7

By the time they reached Main Street, Eddie was shaking with exhaustion and fear. "Hey! Wait for me!" Eddie called, but Harris raced toward his mother's store.

When Eddie came around the side of the building, he noticed Harris's bike tossed near the still-swinging apartment door. Eddie propped his bike against the wall. He grabbed the doorknob and pulled.

Up the stairs to Eddie's right, Harris stood in front of another open door. "This way," Harris said.

At the top of the stairs Eddie found a neatly kept kitchen. Harris dropped his book bag onto a chair at a table opposite the refrigerator. Green gingham curtains hung in the window above the sink. A bowl of fruit sat on the counter. A dishwasher was running quietly.

"Where have you been, Harris? I was starting to worry."

A woman came through a doorway next to the refrigerator with a dripping tea bag in one hand and a steaming mug in the other. She looked about the same age as Eddie's mother. She wore jeans, a tank top, and baubly green beads draped around her neck. When she noticed that Harris was not alone, she said, "Oh, I didn't realize you brought home a friend." Her smile was sweet. Her warm brown eyes matched the few dark strands that ran through her blond hair. "You boys are filthy," she said with amusement. "What have you been doing?"

"Eddie's going to stay for dinner. Is that okay?" asked Harris, quickly changing the subject. He walked over to the sink and started to wash his hands.

"That's fine with me," said Harris's mother, shrugging. "But why don't you call your parents and ask them if it's okay. Do you like leftover meat loaf, Eddie?"

Eddie nodded sheepishly. He hadn't prepared himself to meet Harris's mother, never mind have her invite him to stay for dinner. He felt dirty and intrusive, but when she held out her hand and introduced herself, he realized he was welcome.

"You can call me Frances," she said. "How was the first day, Harris? Who'd you get for homeroom this year?"

"It was fine. I got Dunkleman this time." Harris spun away from the sink and wiped his hands on his jeans, leaving wide wet marks over his pockets. "Come on, Eddie. Let's go play video games. You can call your mom from my room."

"You finished your homework already?" said Frances.

"First day of school. I only have a little bit tonight," said Harris, disappearing around the corner into the hallway. "I'll do it before bed, okay?"

Eddie looked at Frances, who just smiled and waved, shooing him off to follow her son. "Boys," she said with fake exasperation. "Go. Play. It's nice to meet you, Eddie."

"You too," said Eddie, following Harris around the corner.

A few minutes later, Eddie was sitting on Harris's bed, as Harris leaned over his computer's keyboard. "Here," said Harris, typing Nathaniel Olmstead's name into a search engine Web site. Several items related to the author appeared in the search window. *Buy Nathaniel Olmstead books . . . 50% off! Are you an Olmsteady . . . ? Click here!* Harris clicked on the last link, which appeared to be a listing from the archives of the *Gatesweed Gazette.* "Check this out."

On the screen an article appeared, dating from the time of the author's disappearance. Eddie read the first part of it carefully. The article described how the town-wide search party had discovered the statue in the woods.

"After I started getting into Nathaniel Olmstead's books, I came across this article," said Harris, scrolling the cursor to the bottom of the screen. A small box appeared where the article ended, showing a crudely drawn map of the Nameless

Woods. The clearing, the statue, and the lake were specifically marked. "I used this map to find my way. I wanted to see if I could discover anything the search party might have missed."

"What's that there?" said Eddie, leaning forward and pointing at an X that had been marked in the middle of the lake, in the same spot where the water had turned black.

"That's where the police found *evidence.*"

"What sort of evidence?" said Eddie.

Harris scrolled the cursor and read from the screen. " 'When the lake was dredged, police discovered a small metal box. The nature of its contents is being kept secret as the investigation is ongoing. However, an anonymous source has exclusively revealed that this secret evidence has itself mysteriously disappeared.' "

"That is weird!" said Eddie. "What do you think was in the box?"

Harris shook his head. "Listen to this," he said as he continued to read. " 'The disappearance of the evidence was understandable to one eyewitness, who wished to remain unidentified. According to the witness, as the lake was being dredged, a pack of vicious dogs chased the search party from the area. "In all the confusion," said the witness, "anything we found might have been lost. We barely escaped with the seats of our pants intact. It was like something from one of poor Nathaniel's books." ' " Harris stopped reading and turned to look at Eddie.

At the same time, both boys opened their mouths and said, *"The Rumor of the Haunted Nunnery!"*

"I was thinking the same thing when we were up in the woods," Eddie added.

Harris leapt from his chair and ran to the bookcase next to his bed. Eddie could see Harris's alphabetized collection of Nathaniel Olmstead books filling the top row. Harris pulled out a book and flipped through it until he found what he was looking for. Eddie couldn't see the book's cover, but he knew exactly what Harris had found.

" 'Reflected in the water, some of the stars had already changed color, from white to red,' " Harris read aloud. " 'As he watched, they all turned, then began to move. In an instant, they divided into hundreds of pairs of red eyes that watched him from under the lake's surface.' " When he finished, he looked up at Eddie. "The monster lake-dogs."

"Do you actually think that's what we saw?"

"It sure looked like it."

"In the book, the dogs came out of the lake and chased Ronald after he accidentally touched the water," said Eddie.

Harris was quiet for a moment. Then he said, "The water turned black after you threw the pebble at it. Remember? Then we saw those stars. They turned red. Then that thing started to come up onshore . . . just like in Nathaniel Olmstead's book. . . ."

"Right," Eddie whispered.

"The group of people from this article touched the water, too, when they were searching the bottom of the lake," said Harris, closing the book and putting it back on the shelf. "Maybe that's why the dogs chased after them?"

"Maybe," said Eddie. "But I have a different question."

"What do you mean?"

"How does a pack of dogs live underneath a lake?" he said, swiveling toward Harris. "Unless the Olmstead Curse is real?"

Harris blinked at him.

"There has to be some connection between what happened to us in the woods and everything else you told me today," Eddie continued. "The symbol carved into the statue is the same as on the front page of the book my parents found at the antiques fair. The dogs appeared in the lake, just the way Nathaniel Olmstead wrote about them in *The Rumor of the Haunted Nunnery.* And what about the legend of the ghost in the woods—the Woman from the graffiti? Maybe she's . . ."

"What? She's real too?" Harris said into his hands.

Despite what he'd seen in the woods, Eddie felt foolish for thinking something so crazy. He bit at the inside of his mouth and tried not to blush. "It's just a thought."

"If we could read the stupid code, we could sort out what the connection might actually be," said Harris, lifting his face from his hands.

"Totally," said Eddie. "We're on the verge of something really big. But there is something else. . . ."

"What's that?"

"The curse . . . Remember how you said some people in Gatesweed think that the monsters in Nathaniel Olmstead's books are real?"

Harris nodded skeptically.

"Those people don't seem so crazy anymore, do they?" Eddie continued. He thought about the scaredy cop and the tow truck driver, Sam. And Mrs. Singh, the librarian. "Maybe they know something we don't."

Before Harris could answer, there was a knock at the door. The boys jumped as Frances opened the door a crack.

"Dinner's ready," she said. "Hope you're hungry."

Before Eddie got on his bike to ride home, Harris asked him to see *The Enigmatic Manuscript* one more time. Eddie hesitated for only a second before pulling the book out of his bag. After everything they'd gone through today, he felt it belonged to Harris as much as it belonged to him now. He watched as Harris flipped through it, scanning the strange writing.

"What is it?" asked Eddie. "Do you see something?"

"I'm not sure," said Harris, looking up. "Do you mind if I keep this tonight?"

Eddie looked into Harris's eyes, and what he saw there, he knew he could trust. This is what came with friendship. "Okay," Eddie said. "That's cool."

"I'll give it back to you tomorrow," said Harris. "I promise."

Eddie refrained from telling Harris to *be careful* with it, as he got on his bike and waved goodbye.

8

Harris returned the book to Eddie during lunch the next day, just like he said he would.

The day after that, Eddie brought the code-breaker book to school. One small section had caught his eye. It mentioned the history of secret decoder rings—a toy popularized in the 1930s that allowed kids to send encrypted messages to each other. The ring consisted of two alphabets lined up next to each other on two attached discs. To create the secret code, you simply rotated the discs, offsetting the two alphabets, so that the letters no longer matched up. The letter *A* offset by three would become the letter *C*. To solve the message, you simply had to know the offset number.

"Something like this could be the answer to the code in *The Enigmatic Manuscript*," Eddie said.

"Yeah, but that's assuming the code we're trying to

solve is a simple letter puzzle," said Harris, "that this book only needs to be translated, then *bam,* we're done. Mystery solved."

"What do you mean?" said Eddie. "What else would the code be?"

"Well . . . anything, really," said Harris. "When was the last time you read an entire book that had only three-letter words?"

Eddie blinked, frustrated. "Don't you think we should at least try?"

"I guess so." Harris shrugged, unconvinced. "If this decoder-ring thing is the answer, and that's a big *if,* how are we supposed to know what offset number Nathaniel used?"

Eddie shook his head. "We could go through the whole alphabet," he said, "offsetting each letter."

"A through Z?" said Harris. "That's going to be a ton of work."

Together, they spent a week of lunches trying to figure the code out. In the evenings, sometimes, Harris would come home with Eddie, and they would work on their project in his bedroom. Eddie's mother was constantly writing in her notebook at the kitchen table, and his father was always out in the barn, sorting through his antiques, so the house's quiet was suitable for the boys' concentration. They finally made it through the entire alphabet, offsetting the letters one by one.

Unfortunately, it didn't work. The only pattern they could discern was the arrangement of letters into groups of three. Still, they wondered how, or why, anyone would write an entire book using only three-letter words?

Near the end of September, as the leaves finally changed color, and the north wind brought colder, drier air to Gatesweed, Eddie began to feel more at ease in his new school, especially the one day his English teacher introduced his class to Gothic literature. Mr. Weir had asked the class to give a report on a spooky book of their choice. Even though English was his favorite subject, Eddie was still nervous to talk in front of his class. He had prepared the night before by rereading *Whispers in the Gingerwich House,* a book with which he was quite familiar.

His report went well. Eddie only stammered a couple times. No one laughed, so he made it through his speech, then sat down quickly.

After two more reports, someone near Eddie raised her hand.

"Why do we like being scared?" said a voice quietly. Eddie turned around—it belonged to Maggie Ringer, the girl whom Eddie had run into the first day of school. She looked as pale and weird as ever. Her hair was especially stringy, as if she hadn't washed it in days.

"Excuse me?" said Mr. Weir.

"In these stories, the authors are always trying to scare us," said Maggie. "Why?"

Mr. Weir pushed up his glasses and smiled. "Eddie? Can you think of an answer?"

Silence. Then slowly, Eddie nodded. Before he could stop himself, he answered, "So we know what we're up against." All the students looked at Eddie like he was crazy. But he was certain he was right, so he confidently continued. "Nathaniel Olmstead once wrote that most of his stories came from his nightmares," he said, looking at his desk. "He said that we have bad dreams because our brain is trying to protect us." A boy coughed nearby. Eddie wondered if he was making fun of him. "If—if we can figure out a way to beat the imaginary monsters . . ." People started to snicker. Eddie spoke quickly, "Then the real monsters don't seem so scary."

The classroom became very quiet.

"That's why we like reading scary stories," Eddie finished quietly. He folded his hands and stared at the blackboard. "At least, that's what *I* think."

Maggie leaned toward him and said, "So basically, you're saying that monsters are real?"

He made it to the woods before he heard the splashing. . . .

"That's not what I meant," Eddie started to say, but the bell interrupted him and Mr. Weir dismissed the class.

Harris was late meeting Eddie after the last bell to go home. Eddie sat on the stoop outside the cafeteria, looking at his copy of *Whispers in the Gingerwich House.* After rereading the book the night before, he had a strange feeling that there was something inside it to which he should pay closer attention, but he couldn't figure out what it was. He was scanning the beginning of chapter seven, when Viola finds the mirror hidden behind the secret panel in the living room wall, when a shadow crossed his path.

Eddie glanced up and saw Maggie in front of him. Her purple tattered sweater and skinny black jeans looked especially harsh in the slanted autumnal light.

"Can I help you?" asked Eddie, sticking his finger between the pages of his book to keep his place.

She crossed her arms and bit her lip. She wouldn't look at him. Quietly, she said, "I wanted to apologize."

"For what?"

"The scary-story stuff." She tilted her head and shrugged before continuing. "For some reason, every autumn, the teachers bring up the whole Gatesweed ghost and goblin thing. Just wait. Listen to people talking in the hallway and the locker room. I bet you'll hear someone mention the Olmstead estate and how it's creepy and dangerous and we should stay away in case we get cursed and go crazy. *I* live up there. *I'm* not crazy." She paused. "I'm just so sick of everyone talking about it. Obviously, you're not."

Eddie didn't know what to say.

She added, "The class wasn't whispering about you. They were laughing at me. . . . That's what usually happens. I just thought you should know. I'm the class freak, if you haven't heard."

"I don't think you're a freak," said Eddie quickly.

She stared at the book he held in his lap for a few seconds, then said, "So . . . tell me. Are you an Olmsteady?"

Eddie blinked.

"I've seen you carrying his books around," she said.

"You have?" Eddie asked. Had she been watching him? "What's an Olmsteady?"

"Do you really need a definition?" she asked.

Eddie cleared his throat. "Uh . . . no, I guess not." He had heard the term before but hadn't really thought about what it meant. *Olmsteady: one who reads Olmstead.*

"Are you obsessed or something?" She kicked at the stoop with her black boot.

"I wouldn't say obsessed. I just like to read," said Eddie. "Don't you?"

"No. I hate it. But *television* is totally cool." Eddie didn't know what to say. Then Maggie smiled at him. "I'm kidding. I do read. Books about biology and science and cool stuff like that," she said, clearing her throat. "I think those books are terrible, by the way." She pointed at the book in his lap. "Nathaniel Olmstead's."

"Oh," said Eddie, a little bit hurt. "That's too bad. I really love them. They're exciting. Good versus evil. Battling it out. I like being scared. The books make me happy."

"I like science," she said. "There is no good and no evil. There's fact versus fiction. And it doesn't matter who wins. The truth is the truth. . . . Epic tales of good and evil are so unnecessary, you know? Those kinds of battles are fought every single day, right here." Maggie slowly extended her index finger and pointed it at Eddie's forehead, like a gun. "Kapow."

Eddie laughed and quickly moved out of her line of fire.

"I'm Maggie, by the way."

"I know," said Eddie. "I mean . . . I'm Eddie. Nice to meet you."

Maggie smiled. "See you around, Eddie," she said, blowing on her trigger finger as she slinked away. Eddie realized he was staring when he felt someone breathing in his ear.

"She's way too mature for someone like you, dude." It was Harris. "I've seen your pits in gym class. They're totally bald."

"So are yours," said Eddie. He knew his face was bright red.

Smacking Eddie in the arm, Harris said, "You totally have a crush on her."

"No, I don't. I just . . ."

"She's a real witch," Harris whispered. "Be careful. She probably put a spell on you. You might fall in love with her and have little witch babies." Then he started kissing his own hand in a really gross way. Eddie blushed, but Harris looked so ridiculous, he couldn't stop himself from laughing.

Eventually, Harris stopped kissing himself and said, "Mrs. Dunkleman is such a dummy. She made me stay late because I said her skirt looked like a sheep."

"Why'd you say that?"

"Because it did," said Harris, heading toward the bike rack. "Come on, it gets dark early in Gatesweed at this time of year. Let's go to my house. If we can't crack the code today, then at least I'm totally going to kick your butt playing The Wraith Wars on my computer."

Eddie took his finger from *Whispers in the Gingerwich House* and dog-eared the page where he'd stopped reading. The chapter title caught his eye. Chapter Eleven: "The Place Where Stories Are Told." Why did that look so familiar?

When Eddie didn't follow him, Harris called over his shoulder, "Oh, come on . . . don't be a sore loser before we've even started playing the game!"

Eddie waved him quiet. He stared at the book. He didn't want to lose his thought.

"What's wrong?" said Harris.

Finally, Eddie blinked and looked at Harris again. "Have you heard this before?" he said, then read from the page, " 'The Place Where Stories Are Told.' "

Harris stood next to the bike rack. He squinted and looked confused. "Well . . . yeah. 'The Place Where Stories Are Told' . . . It's the phrase that's carved into the stone near the roof of the library. In the middle of town."

Eddie thought about his English class and how Maggie accused him of believing in monsters. *So basically, you're saying that monsters are real?* she'd asked him. Slowly, he began to nod. "Are these words carved into the library because Nathaniel Olmstead wrote them? Or did Nathaniel Olmstead write them because he saw them carved into the stone?"

"I don't know," said Harris. "What do you mean?" He stood over his bike, undoing the chain lock, looking at Eddie as if he were nuts.

"I just have a hunch about something," said Eddie. "My English class today has me thinking about these books again. The statue in the clearing, the symbol on the book, the lake in the woods, the dogs from the *Haunted Nunnery* . . . If they were real, if Nathaniel Olmstead had seen them with his own eyes, then maybe it stands to reason that other parts of his books are real. And not *just* the places that inspired him."

"Are you saying . . . ?" Harris started, then added, "What are you saying?"

"In order to solve *The Enigmatic Manuscript*'s code language, we need the key. Right?" said Eddie, picking up his own bike lock and swirling the numbers on his combination pad. "The answer might be in Nathaniel's stories."

"You think there might be a clue about the code somewhere here in Gatesweed—a clue we might find in one of his books?" said Harris.

"Exactly." Eddie yanked the chain away from his front tire. It clattered against the steel rack with a loud clang before he shoved it into his book bag. "How about we forget the video games tonight?" he said, swinging his leg over his bike and hopping onto the seat. "Let's read a book instead?"

9

Kate was in the kitchen trying to plant the Gremlin's Tongue flower when she heard the baby start crying again. Rolling her eyes, she whispered to the bright purple plant, "I'm sorry, but you're going to have to wait. Someone else wants to be more important than you right now." She went into the hallway and called up the stairs, "Caroline . . . please! The sooner you take your nap, the sooner my headache goes away."

The child's screams echoed down the stairwell, and Kate looked at her watch. Thank goodness—only a half hour until Mrs. James was due back from her meeting. If the baby was sick, Mrs. James would know what to do, and Kate could simply go home. Still, half an hour is a long time to listen to such screaming, she thought as she made her way back up the stairs. Caroline was probably just hungry.

The wet wind slapped leaves against the window at the top of the stairs.

Kate could hear Caroline screaming from behind the closed door. "I'm coming. I'm coming," said Kate. She swung the door open, and immediately the crying stopped. "What's wrong, sweetie?" But the only answer was the storm outside. Kate approached the crib. The blankets were wrapped up in a tangled mess.

Oh no, she's strangled herself, Kate worried as she rushed to the bed and struggled to untie the blankets. When she pulled the sheets away from the mattress, she gasped. The baby was gone.

"You were just *crying," she said, looking around the bedroom. "Where did you crawl to?" When she didn't see Caroline anywhere, Kate leaned against the railing, hanging her head in frustration.*

Something brushed her legs. Startled, Kate leapt away from the crib. "Caroline!" she said, quickly crouching so she could peer underneath the spindly metal frame. "How did you get under there?" But when she looked, there was nothing under the bed except for a few dust bunnies.

Before she could turn around, the bedroom door slammed shut. The sound of footsteps echoed down the corridor toward the stairs.

"That child!" Kate whispered to herself, running toward the door and yanking it open. "Caroline, you are gonna be in so much—" Kate's voice died in her throat.

Down the hall at the top of the stairs a small figure stood, but it was not Caroline. It was about a foot tall and looked human, but its expression was purely animal. The creature was scrawny, naked, and covered in greasy green hair. Its catlike yellow eyes stared at her, and as Kate stared back, it began to emit a quiet growling sound.

When Kate screamed, it raised its claws at her and opened its mouth, revealing pointy brown canine teeth. Then it came at her. Kate didn't even have a chance to close the bedroom door before it—

"You've got to eat something, Eddie," said Dad, from across the kitchen table. "We Fennicks men have a tendency to stay skinny."

Eddie was jerked out of the fifth chapter of *The Curse of the Gremlin's Tongue*—one of his favorites.

"Sorry," said Eddie, looking up. "What?"

"You haven't touched your macaroni," said Mom. "I spent a good two minutes heating it up in the microwave. The least you could do is pretend to like it." She laughed heartily at herself, then blew her nose into her napkin. "Seriously, Edgar, put that book down until after dinner."

Eddie reluctantly closed the book and slid it away from his plate. He pushed his chair against the wall near the refrigerator. A stained-glass lamp hung over the table and cast colorful shadows across the floor.

"Haven't you read it already?" asked Dad.

"Four times," said Eddie.

"Can I borrow it when you're done?" said Mom, getting up and rinsing her dish in the sink. "I really enjoyed the first one you lent me. In fact, *I* started writing a spooky story—the one I was thinking about at the beginning of the month."

"That's great," said Eddie. "I can't wait to read it."

"Speaking of spooky stories, did you ever figure out that weird book we found at the Black Hood Antiques Fair?" said Dad.

"Not yet. But I have a feeling I'm getting closer to an answer." Eddie cleared his throat. He didn't want to tell them everything he had learned about Nathaniel Olmstead, especially since he and Harris had trespassed onto his estate. If they knew how much trouble Eddie had almost gotten himself into at the Nameless Lake, his parents might have asked for the book back. "Me and my friend Harris are working on it together."

Mom closed the dishwasher door and leaned against it so it clicked shut. "That's so nice. Harris seems like a smart boy, doesn't he, honey?" she said, glancing at her husband across the table. Dad smiled and nodded. Before she sat down again, Mom threw her hands into the air. "Darn it! I forgot to serve the spinach!"

Eddie grabbed his plate and his book. Standing up, he quickly said, "I'll eat this in my room, okay?" Eddie hated spinach.

Mom looked like she was going to say no, until Dad grabbed his plate and stood up too. "And I'll finish this in the den." He didn't like spinach either.

~

Later that night, a dream brought Eddie back to the edge of the clearing in the Nameless Woods. The statue of the girl was staring at him from across the circle. He could almost hear a voice calling to him, but he couldn't make out whose voice it was or what she was saying. In the forest behind him, moonlight broke through the trees, sprinkling the small creeping plants with glints of silver, but in the clearing, it shone brilliantly, lighting the statue like a fluorescent bulb. She held out her book, as if she wanted to share it with him. As he stared at her, she glowed even brighter. Her white stone became translucent, and from deep inside the stone, a brilliant blue fire began to flicker. Her eyes darkened. Something moved among the trees directly behind her, and Eddie took a step backward. A horrible stench filled his nose and made him dizzy. He turned to run, but something leapt up from the ground and tripped him. Rolling through the brush to get out of its way, Eddie came face to face with a mouthful of sharp canine teeth.

Screaming, Eddie jolted himself awake. He lay in bed for several seconds, then checked himself to make sure he was not still dreaming. His forehead was clammy, and he felt sick. Moments later, his father peeked his head through the door.

"Nightmare?" he asked.

Eddie tried to swallow, but his mouth was dry. "Uh-huh. Sorry. Did I wake you up?"

"Nah," said Dad. "I was reading. Mom is up late too, scribbling away into her notebook. She's been doing that lots lately."

His father went to the bathroom to get Eddie a glass of water. When he came back, he noticed the book sitting on Eddie's bedside table. On the cover of *The Curse of the Gremlin's Tongue,* a bright purple flower glowed poisonously. Dad flipped the book facedown and turned off the light. "All those scary stories you two have been reading probably don't help."

Eddie knew his father was wrong; the scary stories were the one thing that *would* help.

10

Early the next morning, a northern wind chilled Gatesweed. The previous night's scary dream clung to Eddie's skin, sending him into fits of shivers over breakfast. Outside, the sky was gray and solemn, so Eddie put on his puffy olive coat with the furry hood and set off on his bike.

He found Harris waiting for him, as usual, on the corner of School and Market. Harris was wide-eyed and looked ready to burst with excitement. "I made some progress last night," he said mysteriously.

"What kind of progress?"

"Well, I sort of think you should read it for yourself. *The Witch's Doom.*"

"What about it?" said Eddie, glancing down the street, where the school waited for them patiently.

"There's some stuff in there I think might point us in the right direction."

"Which direction would that be?"

Harris smiled and said, "Nathaniel Olmstead's house." He slung his book bag off his back and opened it. He pulled out *The Witch's Doom* and handed it to Eddie. "Pay attention to the chapter in the basement. You'll see what I'm talking about. If you get a chance to read it during class, maybe we can head up there after school and do some exploring." He pushed away from the curb and swung his bike around into the street. "Come on," he said, calling over his shoulder, "race you!"

Gertie blindly swung her arms around in the pitch-dark basement. Her fist made contact with something hard, and she screamed. But then she heard a smash and a crash and realized she'd only toppled another small pile of dusty junk. Maybe she'd broken the antique clock radio she'd noticed earlier, or possibly it had been the framed photograph of Sojourner Truth. At this point, she didn't really care. Smash everything to pieces, she thought, just let me out of here!

When the echoes stopped ringing against the walls of the cramped stone room, she shouted, "I know you're there!" She was not, in fact, sure that the Watcher had followed her from the woods into the farmhouse, but she figured that if he had, she needed to sound tough, especially now that she couldn't see. She shuffled forward a few inches. It was impossible to tell where she was. If only she hadn't dropped her flashlight into the hole under the stone in the floor!

"I know you can't move if I'm looking at you, so don't even try!" she cried. She couldn't see a thing, but the Watcher didn't know that. Finally, her fingers made contact with cold, wet rock. Following the slab to the right, she was able to locate the ladder, which ran up the wall of the dank basement. She clutched the bottom rung with her fingers. Keeping her eyes forward, she held on to one bar with her hands and put her left foot on the bottom rung. Slowly, steadily, she made her way up. The stone walls dripped with black moisture, and she tried desperately not to slip.

She couldn't believe it had come to this. The only comfort she had was the key she'd taken from the secret compartment in the floor in the center of the room. She hoped that if the monster was indeed down here with her, he hadn't seen her tuck the key in her pocket.

It took all her strength to keep moving up the ladder. Finally, she made it to the top. Reaching up blindly, Gertie could feel the rust-covered door. She pushed at it, but it wouldn't move.

"Fudge!" Gertie whispered to herself. "What do I do now?"

She thought she could hear breathing below her, and when she looked down again, the shadows seemed to move. Gertie screamed. Her voice echoed around the chamber, as she turned and scratched at the rusting metal door above her. Finally, the scream was answered by the turn of the latch and the squeak of the hinges. A sliver of faint light appeared, then the door swung up and out. A face peered at her through the opening.

"Mrs. Thompson!" Gertie said, shocked. "What are you doing up there?"

Gertie's teacher smiled. It was not pleasant. Gertie had never seen Mrs. Thompson look like this before. "Oh, Gertrude. I knew when you found out, you'd act like a nincompoop. You were never very good at tests." Gertie's grip loosened. She couldn't believe what she was seeing. It had been her teacher, all along. The notes. The voices. The nightmares. Mrs. Thompson was the witch. "But this is what was meant to be," Mrs. Thompson continued. "This has always been your destiny, my dear one. Now why don't you climb up here." The witch's eyes darkened. "So you can give me what you have in your pocket."

Something grabbed at Gertie's sneaker, and she screamed louder than before. She swung her foot away from the ladder, but before she could scramble away, the thing's claws tightened around her ankle. Looking down, Gertie could see the terrible face of the Watcher rising toward her from the darkness below.

"Maybe Edgar can tell us?"

Eddie looked up from his book. Ms. Phelps was staring at him; so was the rest of the class. A pie chart was drawn on the blackboard. The students had their math books out.

"Uh," said Eddie. The book he was reading was obviously not math. "I don't know?"

Ms. Phelps came over to his desk. She picked the book up. "*The Witch's Doom*? Detention," said Ms. Phelps, placing the book back on his desk.

Eddie flinched. "What?"

"You may join me after school this afternoon to read up on all the things you've missed this morning, Mr. Fennicks."

Eddie's mouth went dry. He slipped the book into his bag. Detention? Eddie didn't know what to think. What would his mother and father say? And more importantly, would it be dark when he got out?

After class, Eddie found Harris outside of the gym. Eddie's conscience was burning about receiving his first detention ever. He told Harris that their after-school adventure would start later than anticipated. "But before you get too upset, I should tell you that I at least got to read the chapter you wanted me to."

"What did you think?"

"I thought it was totally creepy," said Eddie, "but I don't get why you think it's so important."

Harris raised his eyebrows. "Come on, Fennicks, use your brain. If Nathaniel Olmstead did actually write about stuff he saw with his own eyes, like the lake and the dogs, then we should try looking around his place. Like you said—the answer might be in Nathaniel's stories. In *The Witch's Doom,* the *key* is in a secret compartment in the basement of a farmhouse. . . . Maybe there's something similar in Nathaniel's *own* farmhouse, like the one Gertie found, down in his basement, or under the stairs, or somewhere—any type of place he'd have his characters find stuff."

Eddie understood what Harris was getting at. "If there is some sort of secret compartment, we might find something inside it. A clue of some sort . . . or maybe even the code key itself?"

"Right. That . . . or monsters," said Harris, chuckling.

"Yeah, right. Monsters . . . ," said Eddie, trying to chuckle too, but for some reason, he didn't find that to be as funny as Harris did.

When Ms. Phelps finally let Eddie go, the sun had almost set. He couldn't believe how long detention had been. The sky was a light indigo, and the stars were just beginning to twinkle. It was the start of a crisp fall evening. In a month, it would probably be too cold to ride bikes anymore, but what truly gave Eddie goose bumps was the thought of going up to Nathaniel Olmstead's place in the dark.

He turned right onto School Street. The trees on both sides were tall and wide, their big colorful leaves muted in the shadows. He rode past the post office and the row of boarded-up restaurants at the intersection of Farm Road. The church was dark as he passed it on his right. He left crystallized breath floating behind him as he took a left onto Upper Church, heading toward Center Street. On his right, a few streetlights in the town green eliminated some shadows even as they made more.

Ahead, orange light lit the library from the sidewalk below. Long black shadows stretched from where the window ledges stuck out, making the building look like a storyteller holding a flashlight underneath his chin. Flipping down his kickstand, Eddie parked himself next to the large rhododendrons beside the wide front stairs.

As he waited for Harris, Eddie listened to the evening sounds. The wind rustled the leaves of the trees. Across the park, a car cruised by the darkened bookstore. Where was Harris? The library would be closing soon. Who knew how much longer he'd have before they turned off the lights? The more he thought about it, the more Eddie wanted to wait for daylight to make the journey into the Gatesweed Hills. What was the rush? Nathaniel Olmstead's house wasn't going anywhere, was it?

Wham!

Something banged nearby and Eddie nearly fell into the bushes. He tentatively glanced around and realized he was still alone on the sidewalk.

The noise had come from around the side of the building.

"Harris?" Eddie called. "Is that you?" Peering around the corner, he could see the library stretch all the way to the other end of the block. A small spotlight illuminated a narrow cement walkway that hugged the building. Beside the walkway, a small patch of grass extended to Market Street on the left. No one was there.

Wham!

This time when the noise came, like a gunshot, Eddie felt as if something inside himself had exploded. His breath caught in his throat. "H-hello?" he struggled to say, though at this point, he wasn't sure he wanted an answer.

Creee . . .

A new sound called out—sustained and high-pitched like the wail of a child. Then—

Wham!

Pinpricks danced across Eddie's skin. "Harris, if you're fooling around . . . ," he called out. It felt good to make noise, as if the quiet itself was dangerous. Stepping around the corner of the building, he noticed a railing that jutted out from the library three-quarters of the way back. Beyond the railing, a stairwell led down to the library's basement. A gust of wind whipped along the side of the building, rustling Eddie's hair.

Suddenly, the high-pitched sound came again. That nerve-shattering bang followed a few seconds later.

Eddie jumped.

The sounds were coming from the stairwell. Creeping

along the side of the library, he was finally able to catch a glimpse of the door at the bottom. It opened slightly, revealing a small gap of pitch darkness on the other side.

Creee, sang the rusty hinge. Then the door closed with a soft *ffudd.* The wind hadn't slammed it as hard this time.

His mother's voice ran through his head: *I wish my imagination were half as wild as yours, Edgar. I'd be a bestselling novelist by now.*

Eddie sighed and clutched at his hair. "So stupid!" he whispered to himself. "Someone must have accidentally left it open." To prove to himself that he had no reason to be frightened, he followed the path to the top of the cement stairs, which lay perpendicular against the side of the building. Five steps down, a shadow cut across the stairs where the orange spotlight could not reach. The battered door hid in a dark archway at the bottom. When the wind caught it again, the door opened outward. Only then did the light catch the top of it, before it slammed shut.

Wham!

Even though he now knew what it was, the sound still made Eddie jump. He shook his head and was about to head back to the front steps when he saw something shift in the shadows at the base of the stairs. In the center of a small circular storm drain, dark weedy tendrils grew, flopping in the breeze. Weeds usually wouldn't catch Eddie's attention, but for a brief moment, he was sure he'd seen something else down there as well. Curious, he took a couple steps down. That's when he was certain.

Amid the weedy tendrils grew a small purple flower.

Could it be . . . ?

He felt his bones flood with an excited, electric feeling. Had he really found another of Nathaniel Olmstead's inspirations? If so, might there be some sort of clue at the bottom of the stairs? He cautiously made his way down for a better view. The smell of mildew grew pungent. The bottom step was almost entirely covered in greenish-black slime. Balancing on the edge of the stair, Eddie bent down and examined the flower. About an inch in circumference, it consisted of seven deep-purple velvety petals. Six of the petals clung to a seventh, larger petal. The seventh petal hugged the pistil and stamen before lolling away from the bottom of the flower, its color growing black at its sharp, almost barblike tip.

Creee . . .

The wind opened the basement door slightly as Eddie reached out and touched the stem. It felt like any ordinary flower, but it didn't look like any ordinary flower. Unless he was mistaken, Eddie didn't know of any botany book in which Gremlin's Tongue was actually listed. The only book in which Eddie had ever heard of the flower was Nathaniel Olmstead's. This flower certainly fit the description.

"Eddie?" Harris's voice sounded far away.

Looking up briefly, Eddie called, "I'm down here! I think

I found something!" Suddenly, the wind whipped down the stairs. Inches away, the door slammed shut. *Wham!* Startled, Eddie slipped on the wet moss, and he tumbled face-first onto the ground next to the storm drain.

Moments later, he heard stifled laughter above him. When he looked up, Eddie saw Harris's amused face peering at him over the railing. "Are you all right down there? What the heck are you doing?"

Eddie felt like he didn't have time to be embarrassed. He scrambled to his feet. "You have to see this."

"See what?" said Harris, walking around to the top of the stairs.

"Look," Eddie said, pointing to the storm drain.

Harris came down a few steps. He squinted. "What am I supposed to be looking at?"

When Eddie looked at the drain again, the flower had disappeared. All that remained of the plant were the leaves poking through the slimy metal bars. "But it was just here. . . ."

"*What* was just here?" Harris met Eddie at the bottom of the stairs.

"The flower," said Eddie. "I saw it. . . . It looked just like . . ."

"Like this?" said Harris, bending over. The purple flower lay crumpled near the wall, severed from the rest of the plant. When Eddie saw it, his stomach began to hurt. Harris picked up the flower and handed it to Eddie.

His heart thumping, Eddie held the flower's stem between his thumb and forefinger. It seemed to squirm as the breeze rustled its petals. An awful scent oozed from it—like old food left in a sink of dirty dishes. "Oh no," he whispered. He had a feeling that he'd just made a huge mistake. He squeezed his eyes shut. "I must have accidentally broken the stem when . . ."

"What's the big deal?" said Harris. "It's a flower. Let's get out of here. We've got stuff to do."

"Look closely," said Eddie, holding the flower out for Harris to see.

"If I look any closer, it's gonna poke me in the eye! What are you getting at?"

Frustrated, Eddie took a deep breath. "Doesn't it look like a Gremlin's Tongue?" he said.

Harris took the flower back again. He looked closely, then held it up to his nose and sniffed it. "Like the ones from Nathaniel Olmstead's book?" He wrinkled his nose.

"Am I crazy for thinking that?" said Eddie, embarrassed. "Or is something really strange going on here?" The hinges began to screech again as the door slowly opened. A small dark gap appeared between the door and the frame. The awful smell grew stronger—rotting food mixed with the scent of musty old books.

Creee . . .

"Ugh! They need to fix this thing," said Eddie, glaring at

the door. He brought his foot back, then kicked the door as hard as he could. It swung, but before it could slam shut, it stopped with a dull thud. Something just inside the basement archway cried out in a loud, rough shriek. This new sound was not squeaking hinges.

"What . . . was that?" said Harris.

Before Eddie could answer, the door began to open again, this time more quickly. The gap grew wider as the darkness inside the basement revealed itself to him. Instinctively, Eddie reached out his hand and stopped the door. He began to push it closed.

But something pushed back.

Wide-eyed, Eddie pressed all his weight against the metal door. It slammed shut with another *wham!* Eddie turned around and leaned his bag against it. He tried to speak, but his voice caught in his throat. Harris stared at him. Then the door rattled as whatever was on the other side gave it one hard jolt. Eddie screamed and pressed his back into the metal, his feet sliding on the slippery ground.

The night was quiet for a moment. Harris shook his head. He opened his mouth to speak, but Eddie was thrown forward as the thing in the basement resumed its assault. Harris slammed himself against the door, stopping it from swinging wide open. Eddie recovered, and the two boys pressed it shut with all their strength. The door bounced again and again as the thing on the other side fought back, ferociously trying to escape. Then suddenly it stopped.

After a moment, Harris whispered through his teeth, "You picked that flower."

"Yeah, but not on purpose!"

"So what?" Harris said. "You shouldn't have come down here."

"I was looking for clues to the code!"

"We already knew that some of the things in Nathaniel Olmstead's books were real. Thanks to you, we know the Gremlin's Tongue *gremlin* is real too!"

Eddie knew Harris was right. He shuddered, imagining the creature listening to them from the other side of the door, inches away. They wouldn't be able to stand there holding the door shut forever, especially if the pounding started again. Even though he hadn't meant to pick the flower, Eddie's face flushed in shame. He should have been more careful. Anyone who'd read Nathaniel Olmstead's books knew that to pick a Gremlin's Tongue would release its keeper.

At least now Eddie knew the Olmstead Curse was most definitely real—not that he'd had many doubts after what happened at the lake in the woods. "I don't hear anything," he said. "Is it gone?"

Harris pressed his ear to the door. He listened for a moment, nodded, then said, "Now might be our only chance."

"To do what?"

"Run," Harris whispered, grabbing Eddie's wrist and pulling him away from the door.

Cold air rushed into Eddie's lungs as he took a huge breath and raced up the stairs behind Harris. By the time they reached the top, the door at the bottom had swung open again.

Wham!

Eddie didn't wait to see what had been behind it. Together, the boys ran toward the front of the library, their feet smacking against the concrete sidewalk. They dashed around the corner toward the main entrance. Eddie's own bike sat quietly next to the rhododendrons. He noticed that Harris had chained his bike to the rack. No time to unlock it. As they raced up the front steps, Eddie whispered, "Please be open. Please be open. Please be open." He stretched out his arms to push the front door, but just as he was about to fling the full force of his weight against it, the door swung inward.

"Ugh!" two voices cried in unison, as together Eddie and the person on the other side of the door tumbled to the floor.

Harris scrambled into the library behind them. He slammed the door shut and leaned his weight against it, panting.

After a moment, Eddie noticed that the person on the floor was Maggie Ringer. The books she'd been carrying were scattered across the rug. She winced in pain as she tried to sit.

"I'm so sorry!" Eddie exclaimed. "We were running from—"

Harris nudged Eddie's leg with his foot.

"We were just running. Like . . . for fun?" He struggled to his feet. After he stood up, he offered his hand to Maggie, who still seemed to be in shock.

"Great. Well, next time, it might be more fun for *me* if you look where you're going," she said.

"Are you kids okay?" The librarian, Mrs. Singh, came out from behind her desk. "Why are you standing like that?" she said, looking at Harris.

"We're fine," said Harris, pressing his back against the door. Just then, something slammed against the glass. Harris screamed, then quickly composed himself, bracing the door even harder. His sneakers slid a bit on the rug. He squeezed his eyes shut and said, "Just fine."

"What the heck is that?" shouted Maggie. She pointed at the door, just beyond Harris's feet. Through the glass, Eddie saw what Maggie was looking at. He clutched at his mouth to hold back a scream.

On the library's top step stood a creature unlike anything he'd ever seen. It was about a foot tall. Its skin was bruise-purple. Twists of vine and clumps of dirt and dead leaves littered its greasy green hair, which hung from its head almost all the way down to the ground. Other than this strange cape of thick hair, the creature was naked. The gremlin watched them for several seconds with its yellow catlike eyes, then smiled viciously with its wide greenish lips. It raised its little hand, as if to wave, then brought it down hard against the glass.

Wham!

The door rattled, and once again, Harris screamed.

"A rabid monkey?" said Eddie, feeling foolish even as the words came out of his mouth.

"Does this door lock?" Harris asked quietly.

Mrs. Singh flittered forward, keeping her wide eyes on the thing on the doorstep. "A monkey?" she said, her voice trembling into a weird operatic register. "That is *not* a monkey." She reached around behind Harris and turned the latch. "Excuse me, please," she said. Something inside the door clicked. It was now locked, so Harris stepped away from it.

"Thanks," Harris said to Mrs. Singh. Turning around, he saw the creature staring at him. The thing opened its mouth and tried to bite the glass. Its tiny purple stump of a tongue flipped and flopped like a dissected worm, sliming the door with saliva. Then, from two small pockets on either side of its mouth, several thin green tendrils began to unfurl, their barbed tips tapping and scratching at the breath-fogged glass.

Holding her hand to her mouth, Mrs. Singh uttered a horrified squeak. "I'm calling the police!" she cried, running back toward her desk.

The creature smacked the door with its hand again. This

time, the glass cracked a bit. The thing's mouth-tendrils squirmed to the edge of the door, as if searching for a way inside. The three kids scrambled away.

"That is *not* a monkey," Maggie repeated.

"What are we going to do?" said Eddie, glancing toward Mrs. Singh. "We've both read *The Curse of the Gremlin's Tongue*, Harris. You know the police won't be able to help us."

Harris shook his head in frustration. Then his face lit up. "You're right!" he said. "The police can't help. But you can!"

"Me?" said Eddie. "How?"

"You know how! You were the one who picked the flower. He wants to eat *you!*"

Eddie felt nauseated. "So? That's not a solution! He *can't* eat me!"

"I know that. We won't let him," said Harris, pulling Eddie away from the door. Maggie stayed behind, fascinated by the little monster who continued to watch them from the other side of the glass. "You picked the flower. Only you can send him away. Don't you remember how?"

Eddie racked his brain. He knew the answer to this question. He'd only just reread the book a day ago. The answer hit him. "Right!" said Eddie. "I've got to speak to him in his own language."

"Exactly," said Harris.

"Hello, Wally?" said Mrs. Singh from behind her desk, holding the phone to her ear. "Come quickly. We've got another problem." She glanced at them and said, "You kids, uh . . . stay calm."

Another problem? Eddie didn't have time to think about what she meant by that. He smiled and nodded at her. "We're calm," he said, then quickly turned back to Harris. "I need to put the flower under my tongue," he whispered. "That way, he'll understand what I say."

Maggie spun around and shouted, "What sort of craziness are you two talking about?"

Ignoring her, Harris said, "So where is the flower?"

Eddie felt his stomach drop to the floor. The flower! Had he dropped it? "I don't know," he whispered.

The creature whacked the glass again. The crack grew, spidering out nearly four inches.

"Hurry!" Harris cried. "Check your pockets or something!"

Eddie shoved his hands into his jeans pockets. Save a few pieces of gritty lint, they were empty. Then he searched his coat pockets. When he reached into the one on the right, he felt something small and soft crumpled at the bottom. Cautiously, Eddie pulled out his hand. In his palm, the flower lay, crushed into a little ball. He must have shoved it in there at the bottom of the stairs.

"The flower is ruined!" said Eddie.

Outside, the creature made a shrieking sound. His eyes went wild. His nostrils flared. He banged the door again. This time, the glass shattered. Pieces of it flew onto the rug. The thing's mouth-tendrils skittered nervously across the threshold. Maggie screamed and dashed away from the door. She ran behind Mrs. Singh's desk. The librarian shouted at the gremlin, who was now crawling through the smashed hole in the door, "Shoo! Get out of here!" Then she turned her attention to Eddie and Harris. "Boys! Get away from there!" She motioned for them to join her and Maggie behind the desk.

Eddie almost wanted to start laughing—he knew that hiding behind a desk wouldn't stop the monster.

"Do it anyway," said Harris, ignoring Mrs. Singh. "Put it under your tongue."

"But—" Eddie began to protest.

"It can't hurt!" cried Maggie. She sounded terrified and confused. Eddie knew she had no idea what was going on, yet she might be right.

Standing amid the shards of broken glass, the creature flashed its hideous teeth. Suddenly, it scrambled forward, reaching for Harris's ankles.

Instantaneously, Eddie shoved the crumpled flower into his mouth and swished it under his tongue. It was dry and gritty and tasted like mold. Eddie wanted to throw up, but he managed to keep from gagging.

He meant to shout *STOP* at the creature, but when he opened his mouth, what came out was something totally different. A deep, resonant voice, completely unlike his own, burst from his throat: *"HEST-ZO-THORTH!"* The sound of it shook the room, unsettling the dust from the highest bookshelves. Shocked, Eddie covered his mouth, afraid to open it again.

"It's working," said Harris, shaken a bit himself.

The creature froze several inches from the spot where Harris had been standing a few seconds earlier. It stared at Eddie, as if in surprise, waiting for further instructions. It retracted the tendrils back into its mouth with a loud slurp, like someone messily eating a plate of spaghetti. Eddie didn't know what to do next. The flower seemed to squirm under his tongue, as if trying to escape his own mouth. If Eddie didn't keep speaking, he knew the flower would somehow manage to spit itself out, and the creature would continue on its path toward its terrible meal. He tried to remember what Kate, the character from Nathaniel Olmstead's book, had said to her own gremlin when it had attacked her and the baby during the thunderstorm.

I meant no harm. Please forgive me. Leave us in peace.

Or something like that.

Eddie tried to speak, but the strange voice inside his mouth again spoke its own words instead, *"NO-KOWTH JA-WETH THUN-E-ZATH! SAHWL-KA PA-TEP ZHEP-TA! OM-VHEM HEPATH!"*

The little creature listened, quietly penitent, then hung its shoulders in outward defeat. It almost seemed to roll its eyes as it trudged toward Eddie, stopping a foot in front of him, holding out one hand. Eddie looked at it, unsure of what to do. The creature shook its hand at him, its palm facing up like a beggar asking for money.

"I think it wants the flower back," whispered Harris from a few feet away.

Eddie nodded. He spit the soggy flower into his palm, then very carefully bent over and handed it to the creature at his feet. The thing snatched the flower from Eddie and grumbled something quietly under its breath. Then it turned around and angrily kicked pieces of broken glass as it slunk back toward the library's entrance. After it crunched through the hole in the door, the gremlin spun around quickly and glared at them. Finally, it popped the flower into its own mouth, gave a brief bow, and, before any of them could comprehend what was happening, disappeared.

Silence shrouded the library—until someone behind the librarian's desk sneezed. When Eddie turned around, he saw Maggie holding her sleeve up to her nose. Both she and Mrs. Singh stared in awe. Eddie felt as confused as they both looked, yet he still felt the need to offer some sort of explanation. From outside, the sound of a siren grew as a police car approached. "That was . . . uh . . . that was . . ." But he couldn't think of anything to say that would help them understand, so he joined them in their astonishment. "That was . . . weird," he choked out. "Wasn't it?"

When Wally showed up and saw the damage at the library's entrance, he shook his head and began to write notes onto a small pad. In a low, accusing tone, he asked the boys what had happened. Still hanging back, Maggie stared at the two of them curiously. Harris and Eddie explained that they were about to ride their bikes around the park when the creature attacked them in front of the library. The cop listened patiently, and when Harris finished his statement, he took Mrs. Singh aside and spoke with her privately behind the circulation desk.

After Wally finished taking Maggie's statement, the boys walked their bikes back across the park toward the bookstore. Every dead leaf that skittered across the path made Eddie's skin crawl. The bust of Dexter August stared at him with hollow eyes.

"I'm surprised Wally didn't take us into the station for questioning," said Eddie.

"Mrs. Singh looked pretty freaked out," said Harris. "He'll probably stay with her until she closes up."

"How nice of him," Eddie said with a smirk.

As they crossed the southern hemisphere of Center Street, they agreed that their trip to Nathaniel Olmstead's place was more important now than ever. But they decided to wait until tomorrow, when they could be more prepared, when the afternoon light would provide a better sense of security . . . and when they weren't jumping at every stray sound.

They stopped on the sidewalk in front of The Enigmatic Manuscript. Eddie watched Frances's silhouette float past the lighted windows upstairs.

"Are you gonna be okay going home by yourself?" said Harris. "Do you want me to ask my mom to drive you and your bike home?"

"No. It's a short ride. I think I'll be fine," said Eddie, hitching his book bag up onto his shoulders. "That is, if I don't stop to smell the flowers this time."

Harris laughed and shuddered as he said, "Yeah, right. The ugly purple ones anyway."

When Eddie arrived home, he found his parents in the living room. His father was nestled on the sofa, reading *Antiques Magazine.* Eddie's mom sat next to her husband, scribbling furiously in her notebook. She glanced up when Eddie came through the door.

"Hey, there!" said Dad. "We were wondering where you were! You had us worried."

Eddie turned red, wondering how to respond. Detention after school . . . monsters at the library . . . followed by police questioning? There was no way his parents would understand.

"Yeah, I'm sorry," said Eddie, sighing and dropping his book bag on the floor. "It's been a crazy day. I promise, next time I'll call."

"You'd better." Mom smiled. "Glad to see you made it home in one piece."

Eddie nodded and said, "Me too."

11

In school the next day, Eddie heard his classmates whispering to each other. He wondered how the rumor had spread so quickly that he'd held a flower under his tongue and spoken a strange language to a monster in the library. How many of his classmates had seen something similar in Gatesweed? Eddie tried to ignore the kids who looked at him funny. He had more important things to worry about than a few people who thought he was a freak.

As the clock ticked toward the final bell, Eddie felt his hands start to go numb. Part of him was excited to see Nathaniel Olmstead's house from the inside, but another part of him was terrified. As the past few weeks had proven, Gatesweed was a weird place, and the possibilities for encountering danger were much greater than they'd been in Heaverhill. Having now seen a gremlin, the dogs, and the creepy Watching Woman graffiti, Eddie worried more than ever about Nathaniel Olmstead's fate . . . and his own.

Eddie and Harris met at the bike rack after school. In his book bag, Eddie had brought a flashlight in case the house was dark, a hammer in case they needed protection from any strange creatures, and, of course, *The Enigmatic Manuscript.*

Before they unlocked their bikes, Harris reached into his bag and showed Eddie everything he'd brought too—a flashlight, a notebook, a pen—but when Harris revealed the final item that he'd tucked into his backpack that morning, Eddie couldn't keep from laughing. In his hands, Harris sheepishly held a small bent piece of wood that had a smiling white kangaroo painted on it. "My mother got it as a gift from a customer," he explained.

"That's nice, Harris, but what are we going to do with a boomerang?" said Eddie.

"Hit something," said Harris sharply. "It's better than a stupid hammer. At least I can throw a boomerang."

"Right. But let's hope you don't need to," said Eddie.

Twenty minutes later, they'd made it to Nathaniel Olmstead's estate. They laid their bikes near the road, climbed through the hole in the fence, and hiked up the long driveway. The sun sat low in the sky, painting the long cirrus clouds pink.

Once the boys reached the top of the hill, they walked

around the corner to the back door of the house. It was nailed shut with a few horizontal planks of wood. "On the count of three," said Harris, clasping the middle board in his hands.

Eddie glanced over his shoulder, making sure no one, or nothing, was watching, but the hillside was empty. The orchard trees bristled as the breeze plucked at their barren branches. Eddie imagined the statue standing alone in the woods. The thought of her made him nervous.

"One. Two. Three!" said Harris. The wood ripped clean away from the nails holding it in place. It left a two-foot gap between the top and bottom board. Inside the gap was the doorknob. Harris turned it and pushed. The door swung open with a soft squeak.

Without hesitation, he lifted a leg and carefully stepped over the bottom board. He gripped the door frame, ducked his head under the top board, and swiveled the rest of the way inside. Eddie followed, swinging his first leg through, then his head and body. When he lifted his other leg over the bottom board, a nail caught his pant cuff. He fell face-first into Nathaniel Olmstead's kitchen with an *oomph.* It didn't quite hurt, but it took him a moment to catch his breath. Behind him, Harris quietly shut the door.

"Careful there," said Harris.

"I'm okay," said Eddie as he stood up. Only then did Eddie realize he was actually inside Nathaniel Olmstead's house. His heart was racing, for so many reasons. "Wow," he whispered, and glanced at Harris, who looked as fascinated as Eddie felt. Even though the afternoon was sunny outside, inside the house was dark. Both boys reached into their bags, took out their flashlights, and flicked them on.

"Characters in Nathaniel Olmstead books are always checking under rugs and knocking on walls in case there are hollow spots," said Harris, stepping forward into the gloom. "Keep your eyes open for stuff like that."

Eddie made his eyes really wide and said, "I will."

Harris chuckled nervously.

They wandered to the doorway of the crumbling dining room. Heavy curtains hung over all the windows, shutting out the light. Harris's flashlight crisscrossed the floor and sent rainbows leaping toward the ceiling and walls. A small chandelier had crashed onto the circular table in the center of the room, scattering its crystals across a damp and molding rug.

In awe, the friends silently wandered through the dining room into the long room at the front of the house. The ceilings were so low that Eddie wondered if Nathaniel Olmstead ever bumped his head. They shone their flashlights everywhere, in case something was hiding in a dark corner. The light painted the shadows with circles of white.

The house was a mess. Strange old stuff had tumbled every which way, as if the place had been plundered by thieves. A sun-and-moon grandfather clock lay on its side next to the front window. Its smashed cogs and winches were rusting as time pulled itself away from this place. An entire bookshelf was filled with spindly black antique typewriters whose wiry black keys seemed to have been wrenched apart by violent hands. Eddie desperately wanted to take one home to show his father, but he kept his hands to himself. A dusty globe had fallen onto a stained velvet couch. Victorian statues of sad and dramatic women nestled behind jumbled stacks of books on the floor.

"Where the heck is the basement?" said Harris. "I don't see a door anywhere."

"Check the floor," said Eddie. "That's where Gertie found the hatch."

They continued to search. The house was bigger than it looked from outside. Eddie wondered if Nathaniel Olmstead would have disapproved of them. Two kids . . . breaking into his house, running from monsters, searching for answers . . . No, thought Eddie, Nathaniel Olmstead would not have had a problem with this. He probably would have written this story.

In the corner of the living room, Eddie discovered a doorway that led to a crooked stairway upstairs. He knocked the bottom step with the heel of his sneaker to see if it was hollow like the one Ronald Plimpton found in *The Rumor of the Haunted Nunnery.* But the step seemed to be ordinary. He glanced at Harris, who nodded him forward. Eddie took each creaky step slowly, in case the wood had rotted. At the top of the stairs was a dark hallway. Anything might be hiding in the shadows. He stopped, afraid to move.

Harris scooted past him into the hallway. "Harris," Eddie whispered, "wait!" But Harris turned into one of the bedrooms before Eddie could stop him.

"What's wrong?" Harris said calmly from inside the room.

When Eddie followed hesitantly, he half expected to see the horrible face of the Wendigo hovering outside the window, watching through the dirty glass for trespassers such as themselves. But there was nothing except more furniture, shadows, and dust. He shook his head, convinced he'd officially read one scary story too many.

"This is so cool," said Harris, rushing forward to the big bed. He bounced on it. Dust billowed up in clouds around him. "This must be where he slept."

Reluctant, Eddie joined his friend, removing his bag and lying next to Harris for a few moments, staring at the ceiling, and listening to the creaking of the old house.

Something thumped downstairs. "What was that?" asked Eddie, sitting up and looking into the hallway. Harris sat up too. They listened for a moment.

Then Harris said, "It's probably nothing. . . . Right?"

Eddie hopped off the bed and clutched his bag, feeling the weight of his father's hammer at the bottom. Suddenly, he felt foolish. What good would a hammer be against the gremlin they'd met last night . . . or against something worse?

They wandered back downstairs. In the long living room, a creak came from the wall near the chimney. Together, the boys stepped forward cautiously.

The mantel above the fireplace was dark wood, intricately carved with flowers and fat cherubs frozen in silent song. Underneath it, a pile of birch wood had been carefully arranged upon a pair of imp-shaped andirons. A squat ceramic vase filled with dead, colorless flowers was perched on the left side of the mantel. Eddie's flashlight bounced off the mirror hanging on the wall above the hearth.

The vase crashed to the floor and Eddie jumped onto the nearest chair. His shout was interrupted by Harris's apology.

"Sorry!" said Harris, standing next to the andirons. "My bag knocked it." He bent down and examined the fireplace itself, carefully avoiding the shards of shattered ceramic. Crawling forward slowly, Harris stuck his head through the archway.

"What are you doing?" asked Eddie. He imagined hulking black dogs growling in the corners of the room. But this place wasn't like the woods, Eddie told himself. This was only Nathaniel Olmstead's house. There were no monsters here. Right?

"In *Horror of the Changeling,* Elise finds an envelope in the fireplace," said Harris.

"Oh yeah," said Eddie, leaning forward. He felt as if they were both peering into a gaping mouth. What if the fireplace decided to chomp? He frantically skittered backward, catching his coat sleeve on one of the andirons. Suddenly, the room shook. A loud scraping sound came from inside the chimney, like stone sliding against stone. Eddie yelped, thinking the house was about to collapse—but when he noticed Harris smiling by the glow of the flashlight, he realized that his friend had been right. The back wall of the fireplace had opened up. They had actually found a secret passage! How clever of Nathaniel. It *was* just like one of his books. Eddie had once thought these sorts of things existed *only* in books like Nathaniel's.

"Nice job, Eddie," said Harris as he quickly crawled all the way inside. The opening was about three and a half feet tall and nearly the same width. At the back of the fireplace, the tunnel bent like an elbow. Harris quickly disappeared around the corner. "You coming?" His voice echoed from the shadows.

Crawling on his hands and knees, Eddie felt the soot and grime clinging to his skin. The walls were made of large damp rocks. Moss grew in several places where water had seeped through the cracks. He followed the stone path past the andirons and to the right, where it stretched for a few feet before dropping off.

"Harris?" he called.

"Down here," said Harris.

Eddie peered down to find a small ladder, about six feet high, bolted to the wall. At the bottom, Harris's flashlight bobbed across a stone floor. Eddie gripped the cold metal rungs and lowered himself. The thought of Gertie crawling away from the Watchers at the end of *The Witch's Doom* gave Eddie goose bumps, but he had to keep going.

Another archway greeted him at the bottom of the ladder. He ducked through it and followed Harris's flashlight into a small cryptlike basement with a low ceiling. Spiderwebs draped from the rickety rafters like decaying curtains. Someone had piled a few boxes and stacks of newspapers along the walls. A dark, empty doorway gaped on each side of the room.

"Check it out!" said Harris from across the room. "It looks like some sort of . . . office or something."

A desk with spindly legs sat along the far wall. Next to it stood a tall wooden filing cabinet. One drawer was open.

"Is this where he worked?" Eddie said, trying to calm his frazzled nerves. "How creepy."

"Maybe this is just where he kept stuff he didn't want anyone to find," said Harris. He propped his flashlight on top of the filing cabinet, then reached inside the open drawer. He pulled out what appeared to be a hardcover notebook. He opened it. After looking it over for several seconds, he gasped. "Oh my gosh, Eddie, you have to see this!"

Eddie rushed over to the desk, and Harris showed him the notebook. On the first page, the words *The Ghost in the Poet's Mansion* were written in scratchy penmanship. Underneath the title was the symbol Eddie had found in his copy of *The Enigmatic Manuscript.*

Harris flipped through the entire notebook, shaking his head. "It looks like a handwritten copy of a Nathaniel Olmstead book."

"Someone wrote the whole thing out by hand?" said Eddie.

"That's what it looks like. Just like *The Enigmatic Manuscript.* Only this one isn't in code."

Eddie glanced inside the open drawer. There were more notebooks, their spines facing up. He reached inside, took out another one, and opened the cover.

"Whoa," Eddie whispered.

On the front page were the same scratchy handwriting and the weird symbol Harris had found in the other notebook, but this one was *The Wrath of the Wendigo,* Nathaniel Olmstead's third book. Eddie put the notebook on the desk and picked up another one—*The Revenge of the Nightmarys.* And another—*The Egyptian Game of the Dead.* And another—*The Cat, the Quill, and the Candle.* "Are these notebooks all filled with his original stuff?"

"I guess so," said Harris. He bent down and knocked on the stone floor.

"If he wrote these himself, they're probably worth tons of money," said Eddie.

Harris shook his head. "Yeah, but we're not here for money."

Eddie blushed. "I know that," he said. He reached into his bag and pulled out *The Enigmatic Manuscript.* Opening the front cover, he compared the handwriting on the first page to one of the other handwritten books. "Look . . . Here, where it says *Nathaniel Olmstead* . . . you can see the writing is the same. The same person who wrote *The Enigmatic Manuscript* wrote these books."

"So then it *was* Nathaniel who wrote them," said Harris, glancing up from where he knelt on the stone floor.

"All clues point in that direction," said Eddie. "This is his house, after all. But what does it mean? Why did he write all of his books by hand? And why did he keep them in this secret room?"

"Doesn't look like this room was his only secret," said Harris. "Look at this." He ran his finger around the outer edge of the stone on which he was perched. "This one is different. There's no mortar keeping it in place. Just like the one Gertie finds in *The Witch's Doom.*" He blew at the crevice where the other stones met it. Dirt and dust flew from the crack. When Harris rapped his knuckles against it, the stone sounded hollow. "Help me out." The two knelt down opposite each other, but after trying to lift the stone, they realized that it was stuck. Harris said, "Do you think there's something down here we can use to pull it up?" He glanced around. "What about that hammer in your bag?"

Eddie laughed and unzipped his bag. He reached inside and handed the hammer to Harris. "Hammer one. Boomerang zero."

"Very funny." Harris jammed the claw side of the hammer into the space between the stones. He jimmied it back and forth. It wiggled a tiny bit, but it wouldn't give. "Dammit," he said.

Eddie stood up. "Didn't Gertie use a crowbar in the book? Maybe that, along with the hammer, will do it?"

"If we can find one, sure," said Harris.

They picked through a few boxes in each corner of the room. Eddie searched near the empty doorway and felt that the darkness seemed to stare at him. Icy air crawled across the floor toward him. Frustrated and scared, Eddie scrambled away from the doorway. "This place is giving me the creeps."

"Really?" said Harris sarcastically, glancing up from another box. "Whatever for?" Then he let out a yelp, and Eddie nearly fell over. "I found it!" He knelt near one of the empty dark doorways on the other side of the room, holding a small crowbar over his head.

"You're going to give me a heart attack screaming like that!" said Eddie.

Harris shrugged.

They raced back to the center of the room. Harris hammered the end of the crowbar into the crevice, then, using it as a lever, he was able to lift the stone. After a few seconds, he slid it the rest of the way out of its bed. From inside the hole came a soft wheezing sound—like something trying to catch its breath. Eddie backed away as Harris leaned forward. "Don't tell me you're going to stick your hand in there?" Eddie said.

Harris nodded. "I've got to. There might be an answer inside."

"There also might be a *monster* inside," said Eddie.

Harris rolled his eyes, and before Eddie could stop him, he thrust his arm into the hole up to his shoulder. He scrunched up his face and grunted a bit. "I can feel something. . . . Eww!"

"Is it a monster?" asked Eddie, scrambling away from the hole.

"No. It's not a monster, but, as a matter of fact, it is a little . . . moist." He wrenched himself backward. In his hand, he clutched a small rectangular object. Using his coat sleeve, Harris brushed off the dust and dirt. "It looks like another notebook. Like the ones in the filing cabinet over there."

There was something strange about the book in Harris's hands. Its binding was damp, but somehow inside, the pages were dry. Harris's flashlight gave the book a ghostly glow. He opened the cover.

As Eddie took a closer look, goose bumps rose all over his body. Inside the notebook was the familiar scratchy writing. And on the first page was the same symbol Nathaniel had drawn into the rest of the books.

"*The Wish of the Woman in Black*," Harris read. "I haven't read this one before."

"An unpublished Nathaniel Olmstead book," said Eddie. "Is this one written in code too?"

Harris's hand trembled as he turned the page. He shook his head no. He stammered slightly as he read the first sentence aloud.

" 'In the town of Coxglenn, children feared the fall of night. It wasn't the darkness that frightened them—it was sleep. For when they lay in bed and closed their eyes, *she* watched them.' "

He glanced up from the page and raised one eyebrow. "I wonder why he buried this one under a rock?"

The Wish of the Woman in Black? Why did that sound familiar? thought Eddie.

"Let's get out of here," he said. "We'll finish reading it somewhere else."

"I don't want to have to come back later, in case there's

something else we need from down here." Harris glanced at the book in his hands. "See how far we get?"

"Before what?" said Eddie. He shuddered, sighed, then settled into his place on the cold floor.

Harris read. " 'The ancient people who long ago lived in Coxglenn had built a wall made out of fallen trees, dead bushes, branches, vines, and mud to try and keep her out. It had not worked. Now what was left of the brush barrier was broken by the lane that led into town. Stretching into the woods, its many sharp pieces reached and scratched at nothing, like a blind monster searching for prey. . . .' "

For the next hour, the boys sat in the basement and read the book by flashlight. Every twenty pages or so, whoever was reading handed the notebook off to the other. They both agreed that it was the scariest Nathaniel Olmstead book yet.

The characters in the book seemed to shriek across the blank movie screen in Eddie's head, running in fear from the horrible Woman in Black, whose quiet rage made her arguably the most dangerous creature in the worlds of Nathaniel's books. Whatever—or whoever—stood in her presence would rot slowly from the inside out.

Eddie thought the ending of the fifth chapter was especially scary. He didn't want to stop reading, even though his legs were starting to go numb.

One night, when Dylan lay in bed staring at the ceiling, he heard a noise downstairs. It sounded like something scratching at the walls. He thought it might be a mouse or a squirrel that had accidentally found its way inside. He threw the covers off his bed, put on his bathrobe and slippers, and made his way down the stairs. When he flicked the light switch in the living room, nothing happened. The moon was new, so the room was pitch-black. The scratching continued from the other side of the room.

"Mom?" Dylan called up the stairs. "Dad?" He hoped they would come down, but they did not answer.

A horrible odor filled the darkness. Seconds later, Dylan heard low, inhuman laughter. Something stood in the living room with him, and Dylan could hear its quick, shallow breath. The scratching grew louder and started to inch closer.

He froze. Thinking it was a dream, he pinched himself, but he was horrified to realize that he was already awake.

"Eddie," Harris whispered. "Did you hear that?"

Eddie looked up from the page. He'd become so enthralled with the story, he'd begun to forget where he was. "Hear what?"

"It sounded like . . ." Harris stared off into the shadows through one of the stone archways in the nearby wall. Then he shook his head. "Forget it. Just keep reading."

Eddie allowed himself to stare at the darkness all around him for a few seconds, listening for whatever sound Harris thought he'd heard. The silence of the basement was hypnotic. Finally, he picked up the book again.

Dylan opened the cabinet next to the potted palm and found a candle and a matchbook. He struck the tip of a match, and the spark erupted into the darkness. He lit the candlewick. The flame flickered tenuously before settling into stillness. Looking around the room, he didn't see anything or anyone who might have made such laughter. But the horrible stench grew stronger. It was coming from the wall near the fireplace.

Cautiously, Dylan crept toward the mantel. When he reached the oriental rug in front of the fireplace, he noticed two strange lumps. Bending down, he could see the lumps were piles of familiar clothing. He trembled as he realized what he had found. His mother's bathrobe was wet and soiled. His father's pajamas smelled like rotten meat. Something terrible had happened to his parents. The rug underneath the laundry was dark, and the flickering candlelight revealed an oily sheen. Dylan held his hand to his nose to keep himself from becoming ill. Suddenly, the candlelight was out, and he was thrown into darkness.

"What's that nasty smell?" said Harris, interrupting once more.

Eddie paused. After a moment, he smelled it too. "It's almost sweet . . . like the garbage bins next to the parking lot at school. Where is it coming from?"

"All around," said Harris. Then he looked at the book in Eddie's hands. "Sort of like . . . exactly what's happening to Dylan in the story."

Eddie felt sick, and it wasn't from the stench. He held out the book to Harris. "Y-your turn?" he stammered.

Harris took the book, smiling wearily as he began to read.

In the darkness, something brushed against his leg. Then something pulled his slipper from his foot. Dylan stumbled backward, turned, and ran. He scrambled along the wall to the front door.

Whatever had taken his slipper slithered across the floor behind him. He fumbled with the doorknob, and he flung himself into the night.

The thing chased him all the way down the driveway. Up the road to the right, Dylan saw headlights approaching. He waved his hands, trying to flag down the car. The light grew blinding, and the engine roared louder and louder. He realized it was not going to stop. From the shadows near the end of the driveway, a dark shape leapt at him. He jerked his body out of the way and fell on the far side of the road, just as the car sped by. It missed Dylan by inches. He heard a horrible wet thump and the squeal of tires.

A car door opened. Dylan heard boots on gravel, and a deep voice called, "You all right?"

Dylan stood up and shouted, "Didn't you see me?"

A short, thin man stood next to a pickup truck. "Sorry, man," he said. "I just came off my shift. Didn't expect to see a kid in a bathrobe in the middle of the road at this hour." The man looked down and then shouted. "Aww, geez, what the heck did I run over?" In the middle of the road lay a black lump about a foot in diameter. It was wet and shiny in the truck's headlights. "It's not yours, is it?"

Mesmerized by the lump in the road, Dylan shook his head.

"Some kid is going to be really unhappy tomorrow morning. Poor little thing," said the man, taking a step closer to examine the mess.

The man bent over as Dylan shouted, "Get away from it!" But it was too late. A slick humanlike hand shot out of the wet puddle and grabbed the man's collar. Dylan watched the man's face turn dark and oily, his skin seeming to melt away like wax. Not even his screaming could be heard over the sound of a woman's fierce laughter, ringing across the Corglenn Hills.

Harris tossed the book to the floor. His eyes grew wide and he stifled a small whimper. "I just thought of something. . . ."

"What's the matter?" asked Eddie, sitting up straight.

"The Woman," Harris said, staring at the book.

Eddie's stomach turned to ice. Of course! That's why the title had sounded so familiar. *The Wish of the Woman in Black.*

"Eddie, do you think . . . ?" He didn't need to finish. Eddie had already started nodding.

It was her—the woman from the Gatesweed legend. The ghostly woman the townspeople said haunted the woods. The Watching Woman from the graffiti.

"You know what this means?" Harris continued.

Eddie nodded again. "Nathaniel did write a story about her, after all." Looking around the basement, he felt the shadows pressing on him. He shuddered as he came to a terrible understanding. "Does this mean that the Woman in Black is real? Just like the gremlins and the dogs in the lake?"

Harris only nodded slightly, as if he'd come to the same conclusion. "Maybe people in town *aren't* crazy. Maybe they really *have* seen her. Maybe she *is* watching?"

Eddie took a deep breath, then exhaled, trying to remain calm. He spoke slowly and evenly. "Maybe there's a connection between the handwritten books we found here in the basement and the creatures we've seen in Gatesweed. . . ."

"What kind of connection?" said Harris.

Eddie shook his head. "Maybe he *knew* that some of his monsters were real. Did he think the Woman was real too? Could he have buried this book under the stone because he thought *her* story was too scary?" Suddenly, Eddie had a terrible feeling. "If it was too scary for *him*," he whispered, "then what the heck are *we* doing here?"

Harris continued to stare intently at the book on the floor. "We're doing what Nathaniel Olmstead would have wanted us to. Solving the mystery." He picked up the book again and turned to where he'd left off, but when he flipped the next page to continue reading the story, he yelped.

"What's wrong?" said Eddie, shining his flashlight at Harris.

Harris held his hand in front of his face to block the light, but he didn't hesitate before showing Eddie what was on the next page.

P B Z D Y F R H V J W L U

A Q C O E T G S I X K N M

"No way," said Eddie. Quickly, he picked up *The Enigmatic Manuscript* from the floor. Opening the cover, he compared the strange writing to the letters they'd just found in *The Wish of the Woman in Black.* After a few seconds, he said, "Why would Nathaniel Olmstead have written the code in this book too?"

"I'm not sure." Harris pressed his lips together and flipped one more page. He looked distressed. He held up the book and showed Eddie. The rest of the pages were blank. "This is where it ends. *The Wish of the Woman in Black* is incomplete. He buried the book without finishing it."

Eddie felt empty. "That's everything he wrote?" he said. "But how does the story end? And why doesn't he actually explain what the stupid code means?" He tossed *The Enigmatic Manuscript* on the floor next to the hole, where it landed with a soft *whap.* "We were so close to finding the key. What are we supposed to do now?"

Something on the other side of the room sneezed, and

the boys froze. The noise had come from the doorway near the secret fireplace entry.

After a few seconds of silence, Eddie whispered, "H-hello?"

Harris seemed to come to his senses and suddenly whipped his flashlight toward the doorway. "Who's there?" he said. Then he reached into his bag and pulled out his boomerang. If Eddie hadn't been so terrified, he might have laughed at the image of the kangaroo shaking in Harris's hand.

Harris's light illuminated a shapeless dark figure. It scrambled backward against the wall near the ladder. Its clothes were black. Its white hands clutched at its pale face.

Was it the Woman in Black? Had she finally come after them, to turn them into piles of black ooze just like she had done to the characters in Nathaniel Olmstead's book? But then Eddie quickly realized he was wrong. The Woman in Black would never cower from her victims.

"Would you please stop shining that in my eyes?" asked the figure.

"Who are you?" asked Harris. His fear seemed to drain away as he stood.

The figure brought her hands away from her face, squinting at the light, as Harris ignored her plea and continued to shine it at her. Finally, Eddie reached out and lowered

Harris's arm so that the beam of light fell on the floor at her feet. "It's Maggie," said Eddie. "Maggie Ringer."

"You scared the hell out of us!" Harris screamed. His voice echoed through the underground chamber. He raised the flashlight and shone it at her face again. "What are you doing here?"

"I could ask you the same question," said Maggie harshly. She stared at them defiantly, flaring her nostrils like a cornered animal. After a few seconds, she lowered her voice and said, "If you take that light out of my eyes, I'll answer."

Harris grunted and lowered the light again.

"I was coming home from school this afternoon," said Maggie, "riding my bike up Black Ribbon, when I saw you guys ahead, crawling through the gap in the fence at the bottom of the Olmstead driveway. I just wanted to find out where you were going, so I followed you."

"You shouldn't have," said Harris, carefully placing *The Wish of the Woman in Black* next to where *The Enigmatic Manuscript* lay on the floor. "This is a dangerous place."

"Then why are *you* guys here?" asked Maggie, even though she looked like she already had an idea.

"It's a secret," Eddie said. He felt his face flush, imagining the looks he would get in school tomorrow if anyone found out what they had been doing here. "You can't tell anyone."

"How long have you been down here?" asked Harris. "That stench. Maybe it was . . ."

Maggie blinked at him. "What, me? Thanks, but no. I smelled it too, when I finally crept down the ladder a few minutes ago. I was listening to you guys from the mouth of the fireplace. For a while I could hear you really well, but then you started talking quieter. So I came closer."

"Maybe the stench really *was* from—" Eddie was interrupted when Harris poked him in the arm.

"The Woman in Black?" said Maggie. She shook her head. "I already knew that you were up to something really strange, but this beats all. Codes? Monsters? And all these books you were talking about? Whatever you're doing, it's creeping me out."

Harris said, "That's why you shouldn't have followed us."

"I'm sorry!" she said angrily. "But what I saw in the library last night was totally crazy. I'd been doing my homework, and then you guys showed up with that . . . *little monster* following you. And then . . . those weird words you spoke, Eddie. You can't expect me to just be like, *Oh, okay, whatever . . . duh!*"

"It's still none of your business," said Harris.

"Maybe we should go," suggested Eddie.

"Good idea," said Harris. "You and me will finish this *later.*"

Eddie bent down and picked up the books from the floor,

steering clear of the dark hole. It almost seemed to sigh at him as he backed away from it.

Harris stomped toward the doorway where Maggie stood. "Excuse us, please!" he said, brushing past her and stepping onto the bottom rung of the ladder, which was bolted to the stone wall.

When Eddie followed, Maggie looked at him and said, "I said I was sorry."

"It's okay," whispered Eddie. "It's hard to explain it all right now." As Harris climbed up the ladder in front of him, he turned around and scowled.

Once they crawled from the mouth of the fireplace, the three kids went out the back door. The sky was black, and a big moon peeked through thick clouds on the horizon.

"Wait for us!" Eddie called as Harris disappeared around the corner of the house. Eddie clutched the two books, one in each hand. He slipped them into his bag, then swung the strap over his right shoulder. Maggie walked silently next to him as they made their way across the hill and into the pocket of trees at the top of the long driveway.

"I'm sorry to interrupt," whispered Maggie as she ran forward to tug on Harris's coat sleeve. He spun around and threw her a nasty look.

As Eddie caught up to them, his flashlight lit Harris's sooty face from below. Harris appeared downright evil. Noticing the frightened look on Maggie's face, he softened. "What's wrong?"

Maggie glanced back toward the house. "Do you guys get the feeling we're being followed?"

"You're being paranoid," said Harris, though he sounded uncertain himself.

"No," said Eddie, "I feel it too." The thought of the monsters from Nathaniel's books hit him in the back, and he spun around, searching the shadows for movement. One of

the large clouds had moved across the moon, so there was little light to see by. The woods at the top of the driveway were quiet and still. Eddie fought the temptation to call out into the darkness. He didn't want to be answered.

"What was that?" said Harris, looking over Eddie's shoulder.

Then they all heard it. From somewhere in the woods, a few feet up the hill, came the sound of fluttering—a wing, a leaf, a piece of paper. Bumps rose on the back of Eddie's neck, as if an icy breeze had suddenly blown past.

"Is someone there?" Maggie asked, a little too loudly. She had turned even whiter than usual. Then she fell backward, tripping over her feet. Eddie rushed to help her, but Maggie's eyes were fixed on the house, still partially visible through the trees. "Look!" she said. When Eddie turned around, he too almost tripped.

At first, he saw nothing unusual—trees, shadows, passing moonlight. Darkness and more darkness. But then, Eddie's eyes adjusted. It seemed that the empty spaces between the trees had filled, as if each black shadow solidified into a long, tall body. Eddie sensed slight movements, as if the forest itself were letting go of something it had been holding back.

Leaves crunched as a breeze rustled the forest floor.

Moving away from the empty spaces between the tree trunks, with almost imperceptible fluidity, the shadows revealed themselves as dozens of cloaked beings. Without having taken a single step, the beings materialized where Eddie, Maggie, and Harris stood at the top of the driveway. Under each hood was a stark white face. Their lips were pulled back, and what might have been a smile on any other living creature, here, was anything but.

Eddie rubbed at his eyes, then whispered, "It's happening again."

Harris stepped forward, clutching the boomerang. "Watch out, you guys," he whispered to Eddie and Maggie, before calling to the creatures, "Leave us alone!" Harris pulled his arm back over his shoulder, then, with a quick flick, whipped the small piece of wood forward and sent it flying. Eddie was almost impressed as he watched the boomerang soar into the shadows, but the feeling disappeared when one dark creature swiped at it with a clawed hand and the boomerang simply vanished with a soft *whoosh.*

Suddenly, both of his hands were yanked backward, by Maggie on one side and Harris on the other. They pulled Eddie farther down the path, and the three kids ran.

Every tree they passed seemed to let go of another empty space that turned into a hooded creature. They appeared at every angle. Eddie nervously bit the inside of his lip, so hard he tasted blood.

Bare branches extended across the driveway, as if trying to scrape at them. Harris shouted as his cheek split open. Maggie screamed as she lost a tangle of hair. Eddie was sure the trees themselves were in on it. He heard the left side of his coat split down the back as something ripped clean through it.

Eddie's bag slipped off his shoulder and toppled into the brush. Harris and Maggie continued to dash down the driveway, the flashlight's beam bobbing in the inky shadows. "Wait!" Eddie called. But it was no use. Skidding to a clumsy halt in the middle of the overgrown driveway, Eddie spun around. His bag lay on the forest floor, obscured by a small pile of leaves.

He started to scramble toward the bag when he realized that an enormous figure stood over him, cloaked in a filmy transparent shadow like black gauze. Eddie looked up into its face. Its swollen, piglike eyes dared him to look away. Its mouth grew wide as Eddie watched, showing him sharp teeth set in a round skull covered with pasty greenish-white skin. Eddie tried to scream, but nothing came out. The wind blew through the treetops, and like a candle flame the figure wavered before materializing again. Eddie saw the rest of the creatures behind the one towering over him. They were scattered throughout the forest and up the driveway like chess pieces, waiting and watching.

"Eddie!" Harris and Maggie called to him from down the hill.

"Urgh," was all Eddie could muster. His tongue felt like old parchment. His voice was gone—fear had sucked it from his throat. He waited for the creature to descend upon him, but standing there, he realized it had frozen in place. As he struggled to swallow the cold night air, Eddie stared into the horrible face of the monster, and an idea began to fill him with courage.

Since moving to Gatesweed, Eddie had met the dogs from *The Rumor of the Haunted Nunnery* and encountered the gremlin from *The Curse of the Gremlin's Tongue.* Eddie knew that he was now looking at the Watchers—the Witch's hench-creatures who had followed Gertie from the woods into the basement of the old farmhouse. Yesterday afternoon, Eddie had read about them in *The Witch's Doom.* They were real too. And he knew how to beat them.

"Eddie!" Harris's and Maggie's voices shocked Eddie out of his stupor.

He shouted, "Stay where you are! Don't move. I'll be there in a second."

Keeping his eyes focused on the Watcher in front of him, Eddie reached forward and picked up his book bag. He slipped it onto his shoulder and took a step backward. The

Watchers remained frozen, tied to their shadows, unable to move. As Eddie inched farther away, they stopped grinning. Once he was twenty feet away, they closed their eyes and opened their mouths in anguished, silent howls. Eddie tried his best not to stumble over the rocky path. All the creatures needed was for him to look away for a moment. He concentrated, then called to his friends to direct him.

Walking backward all the way down the driveway, he eventually found Harris and Maggie crouched behind a tree near the hole in the iron fence. Even though he could no longer see the Watchers through the dense trees, he knew they must still be at the top of the hill, so he kept staring in that direction. He was too frightened to even risk blinking.

"Come on! Let's go!" said Harris as Eddie finally made it to the fence. "What are you doing?"

"Can I borrow your flashlight?" said Eddie. Harris handed it to him with a frustrated groan. Eddie shone it into the woods up the hill with a sigh of relief. "They're allergic to light," he explained. "They can't follow if you watch them," said Eddie, staring up the driveway.

"What do you mean—they can't follow you if you watch them?" said Maggie. "Is that how you got away? You walked backward through the woods? How did you figure that out?"

Eddie nodded. "It's how Gertie got away in *The Witch's Doom.*"

"Of course!" said Harris. "I remember those things! They were really horrible."

"The Witch's Doom?" said Maggie. "I don't get it. Are you saying those things came from a Nathaniel Olmstead book?"

As Eddie nodded yes, the flashlight splashed her face with a ghostly glow from underneath. Even with a smudge of dirt on her nose, she looked so pale that, for half a second, he thought she looked like the statue in the woods, but when her voice wavered, he knew she couldn't be anyone but herself. She looked between the two boys skeptically, as if they might be playing a joke on her.

Maggie thought about that for a second. Even though she still looked confused, she nodded, seeming to understand what they were saying. "Do we have to walk backward all the way back home?" she asked. "My dad'll kill me if I bring home several dozen giant shadowy demons."

Despite everything, Eddie laughed. Harris joined him.

"I don't think they'll follow us," said Eddie. "They need the shadows, and even though it's only half-full, the moon is probably too bright outside of the woods. In the book they only appear when it's very dark out. But just to be sure, I'll keep my eyes behind us until we get somewhere safe. You guys can guide me."

"My pleasure," said Harris, brushing aside the vines that covered the hole in the fence. Eddie stumbled backward as

Maggie and Harris steered him through. He prayed that the Watchers were no longer watching.

They picked up their bikes and walked them up the hill to Maggie's house, where her father begrudgingly agreed to pile everyone into his pickup for a ride back into town. As they passed the entrance to Nathaniel Olmstead's overgrown driveway, the moon returned from behind a small bank of clouds, and Eddie finally felt safe. He knew the Watchers would never set foot past the shadows where the trees ended and the moonlit asphalt began.

Eddie was sitting at his desk to distract himself with math homework, a task he expected would be nearly impossible after the evening's events, when his mother knocked on his bedroom door. She'd reheated his dinner and brought it up to him, along with the cordless phone.

"It's for you," she said, resting the large antique silver platter on the comforter folded at the end of his bed.

"Thanks, Mom," he said. She kissed his cheek before heading into the hallway and closing his bedroom door.

"Hey!" Harris said. He sounded exhausted. "Are you okay?"

"I'm fine. How 'bout you?"

"Freaked out," said Harris. "Those things were scarier than the dogs from the lake. Scarier than the gremlin."

Eddie silently noticed that he didn't include the Woman

in Black. Despite the horror of meeting the Watchers, he knew they both understood that meeting *her* would be worse.

"Where did they come from?" said Eddie.

"I'm not sure," said Harris. "In *The Witch's Doom,* the old woman tells Gertie that legend during the town meeting, remember? She says the Watchers haunt the woods once the sun goes down."

"Right," said Eddie. "Maybe the same thing happens up at the Olmstead estate."

Harris was quiet. Eddie could hear him breathing over the phone.

"What's wrong?" Eddie asked.

"I was just thinking . . . if those things live in Nathaniel Olmstead's woods now," said Harris, "did they arrive *before* or *after* he left?"

Eddie shook his head. "Let's not think about that," he said, changing the subject. "I feel like we're closer than ever. Did you get a chance to look at the code in the new book? I think it was different from the code in *The Enigmatic Manuscript.* Why don't you check?"

Harris paused before answering. "I don't have the books. *You* have the books."

"Oh right," said Eddie. "I forgot." He grabbed his open book bag and dug through his notebooks and folders.

The books! Where were the books?

A terrible thought flickered through Eddie's head. When

he'd dropped his bag, had he lost the books? Everything had happened so quickly, it was difficult to remember if the bag had seemed lighter when he'd retrieved it from the pile of leaves. He'd been so concerned with trying to escape those *things.*

He imagined the books sitting in the middle of Nathaniel Olmstead's driveway—a place he had hoped to avoid for quite some time.

"Uh . . . ," he struggled to say. His face began to sting. He emptied the bag, but the only thing remaining was the big hammer at the bottom, which he quietly shoved in the back of his desk drawer.

"Eddie? Are you there?"

"Yeah," Eddie whispered. "I'm here . . . but the books are gone."

12

Every time someone slammed a locker door the next day at school, Eddie felt like jumping out of his skin. His heart raced when Ms. Phelps asked him a question about ratios. Out of the corner of his eye, Eddie thought he saw someone watching him in the mirror while he washed his hands in the boys' bathroom, but when he turned to look, no one was there. The past couple days had taken a toll on his nerves.

Part of him was relieved that he had lost the books the night before. If it weren't for Harris, Eddie thought he might want to take a big break from anything having to do with Nathaniel Olmstead. But the other part of him felt terrible that all the work they had done so far was gone. Now, even if they were actually smart enough to figure out what the code meant, they couldn't!

They met after third period outside the gym. When

Eddie saw Harris, he gasped. Harris looked terrible. His hair was greasy, his eyes were glazed, and he looked like he'd just crawled out of bed.

"What's wrong?" Eddie asked.

"I couldn't sleep," said Harris. "I kept wondering where we might have lost the books. I know last night you said you didn't want to, but the only thing I can think to do is go back to the house and look for them."

They heard a sneaker squeak on the linoleum behind them. When they turned, Maggie smiled. For the first time since he'd met her, Eddie thought she looked happy to see him. She brushed her dark hair out of her face and hiked her bag up on her shoulder. "Can I come?"

Eddie and Harris were speechless.

"Look," said Maggie, "that was some crazy stuff up there in the woods last night. I can't stop thinking about it." When the boys didn't answer her, she said in a playful tone, "Then I guess it's not really worth showing you what I found."

Harris rolled his eyes. "What did you find?"

"You're not interested. Forget it."

"Maggie . . . ," said Eddie, sounding more pathetic than he wanted to.

"This whole *boys-only* thing is so fifth grade," she said. She smiled again. "Promise you'll let me come, and I'll tell you."

Eddie turned to Harris. Somehow, he was certain what

she had to offer would be worth it. They both nodded. "You can come," they said at the same time.

"Great." Maggie slapped their shoulders. They both winced.

"So tell us. What did you find?" Harris said.

Maggie slipped her bag off her shoulder, reached inside, and dug around. "In the house last night, I overheard everything you said." Harris started to protest, but Maggie interrupted. "Get over it." Harris folded his arms but listened. "After you read that story about that creepy old woman, Eddie, you mentioned something about a code that matched up a couple of books you guys had." She pulled two books out of her bag. "These books, right?"

"Oh, geez," said Harris, turning pale, throwing his hands to the ceiling. "Thank goodness."

"Whoa," said Eddie, relieved.

"Guess we don't really need to head back up to the woods, after all," she said, smiling, and handed the books to Eddie. "You left them in my dad's pickup," she said. "He found them this morning. We were all pretty out of it last night when he gave you a ride home, so I guess you didn't notice that they'd fallen on the floor. Still, if they're so important, you might want to keep closer watch on them."

"We'll try," said Harris, slamming his locker.

The second bell rang. They were all officially late.

"I've got to go," Eddie said, inching down the hall.

"But I solved your code," said Maggie smugly.

Eddie wasn't sure if he heard her correctly, but when he saw Harris's mouth drop open, he figured that he had. The hallways were slowly starting to empty, and Eddie's heart started to race as he realized that the hall monitors would soon be at their stations.

Maggie shoved another loose piece of hair behind one ear and said, "How do you guys feel about cutting class?"

13

Inside the school library, they found a quiet table in the reference section—an isolated spot toward the back of the room, hidden behind several large shelves near the windows.

Maggie took a piece of paper out of her book bag and placed it on the table, facedown, next to *The Enigmatic Manuscript* and *The Wish of the Woman in Black.* She zipped up her black hooded sweatshirt, then pushed her dark, messy hair behind her ears. On her wrist, she loosely wore several black rubber bands, which she adjusted before resting her skinny hands on the table in a businesslike manner.

Eddie remembered that she'd told him about liking science and math. Funny, he thought as he stared at her, in her Goth costume she looked more like she'd be into magic and mystery stories. Maybe she was, but she just didn't know it yet.

"I don't mean to sound like a total jerk," Maggie began,

"but before I tell you anything, I want to know what's going on here."

"Lots of stuff is going on here," said Harris. He picked up *The Enigmatic Manuscript* and tapped its spine on the table. "What do you want to know?"

Maggie thought, took a deep breath, and then said, "Well . . . everything."

Before the next bell rang, Eddie managed to tell Maggie most of what had happened to him since coming to Gatesweed. She spent several seconds silently contemplating his story. Then she turned to Harris and said, "You seem to be a Nathaniel Olmstead expert, so what do *you* think is going on here, Harris?"

Harris smiled and leaned forward to answer. "After everything that's happened to Eddie and me, I'm beginning to think Nathaniel Olmstead's monsters chased him out of Gatesweed." Then his smiled dropped, as he seemed to recall the previous night's events. "Chased him out . . . or something worse."

Maggie and Eddie glanced at each other. "That would mean the monsters in Nathaniel Olmstead's books are *real*," she said.

"When the Watchers chased us through the woods last night, they certainly looked real, didn't they?" said Harris.

"You've heard of the curse. And you *saw* what happened in the library."

"Yeah, but . . ." After a moment, she closed her eyes and shook her head. "There's got to be a rational explanation for all of this."

"Every single thing that's happened to us so far seems to be connected to Nathaniel Olmstead's stories," said Eddie. He opened *The Enigmatic Manuscript* to the front page. "We were hoping this book might give us a clue why." He looked into Maggie's eyes. "You said you solved the code. Please. Will you tell us how?"

Maggie sighed and hugged her rib cage. "Last night, I flipped through the two books," she said. "I remembered what you'd said in Nathaniel Olmstead's basement, Eddie. About the code appearing in both books. You need a code key in order to read it, right? After I stared at it for a while, I had an idea. Since there were only two lines written at the end of the Woman in Black book, I counted the letters. There are twenty-six of them. No more. No less. And they're all different. See? Only one of each." Maggie opened to the last page of *The Wish of the Woman in Black.* Eddie looked at the letters Nathaniel Olmstead had scrawled there.

P B Z D Y F R H V J W L U

A Q C O E T G S I X K N M

Maggie was right. There were twenty-six letters. She sounded as excited as Eddie felt, when she added, "What else do you know that has twenty-six letters?"

Harris nearly toppled over in his chair. "No way!" he said.

Before Eddie was able to yelp too, Maggie reached out and turned over the piece of paper on the table. At the top, she had drawn out the answer for them to see.

P B Z D Y F R H V J W L U
A Q C O E T G S I X K N M

"*A* is below *P*," she explained. "*B* is above *Q*. *C* is below *Z*. And so on. Simple, really. Each letter has an opposite. In the text, he just switched their places. That's his key."

"Did you try it on the code?" said Harris. "Does it work?"

Nodding her head, Maggie pushed the paper toward him. "He broke the words up into groups of three letters. And he doesn't use any punctuation. It's hard to read, but I think he was trying to make it more difficult to find a pattern." She handed him a pen. "See for yourself," she said.

Harris laid *The Enigmatic Manuscript* open and used Maggie's code key as a reference as he started to translate the first few sentences. Eddie drummed on the table as Harris wrote. When Harris gave him a dirty look, Eddie folded his hands in his lap.

Finally, Harris laid down his pen and picked up the paper. It trembled in his hands. He cleared his throat and slowly worked through what he'd written. " 'I have made an enormous mistake.' "

Wide-eyed, Harris glanced up at them before continuing. " 'The creatures have come through the door, Gatesweed is on the verge of catastrophe, and I realize now that it is my fault. The Woman in Black will haunt me until I use the pendant to open the gate for her too, but I can't. I won't. I've seen what she can do. Instead, I must stop her. I fear I may fail, but I have no choice. And so I must write my own story.' "

Harris dropped the paper, his mouth open in shock. "Holy cow," he said quietly, staring at the paper. " 'The creatures have come through the door'? 'Gatesweed is on the verge of catastrophe'? And it was Nathaniel's fault?"

"But . . . what does it mean?" said Maggie.

"It means you were right, Maggie," Eddie whispered. "You're a genius. That was the secret. The key was right *here.* In *The Wish of the Woman in Black.*"

"We've got some answers now, which is amazing, but we also have more questions," said Harris. He glanced at the paper in his hand and read through it several more times to himself. When he was done, he looked up. "Where is this gate he's talking about? And what is this pendant-thingy? And what does writing his own story have to do with anything?"

"And what about the key itself?" said Eddie. "Why would Nathaniel Olmstead have written the code key in this book and then buried it in his basement?"

"He obviously didn't want anyone to find it," Maggie said.

"I have a question about the code too," said Harris. "What about the symbol on the first page, the one that's carved onto the statue in the woods? Pi is part of the Greek alphabet, not ours."

Maggie shook her head. "That's not pi," she said, pointing at the first page of *The Enigmatic Manuscript.* "I think it's Hebrew."

"Hebrew?" said Harris. "Do you know what it says?"

"It doesn't say anything," said Maggie. "It's only a letter called *Chet.*"

"Chet?" Eddie repeated. "Why do you think it's carved onto the statue?"

Maggie shook her head.

Harris thought to himself for a moment before turning to Eddie. "Where did you say your parents found this book?"

"The Black Hood Antiques Fair—a few months ago, I think," said Eddie. "North of the mountains?"

"I wonder how it got up there?" said Harris. "I mean, doesn't it seem like Nathaniel Olmstead would have wanted to keep this book down in the basement with all the other ones he wrote by hand?"

"Only one way to find out, I suppose," said Maggie,

pushing the pen and paper toward Harris. "Better hurry, before someone discovers we're missing."

"Here," said Eddie, pulling out a spiral notebook. "We'll all work at the same time." He laid *The Enigmatic Manuscript* on the table so each of them could see it.

They worked for the next two periods. Whenever they heard someone approach, they scattered, hiding in separate aisles of books. Returning to the table, each of them continued to translate a part of the page. When they were done, together, they would read their parts aloud, before going on to the next page. In this manner, they slowly but surely began to piece the story together.

At first, the book was filled with fairly standard autobiographical information. It was interesting, but as he continued to read, Eddie wasn't sure why Nathaniel felt the need to write his life story in code. Nothing about his reading ghost stories late into the night seemed all that scandalous.

Then Eddie learned something about Nathaniel Olmstead he didn't already know.

From early on, Nathaniel didn't think he had enough talent to be a writer. He never thought his ideas were any good. Saving his allowance each week, he sought inspiration at second-run monster movies in his hometown of Coven's Corner, but afterward, when he went home and took out his notebook, all he could imagine was what he'd seen that afternoon.

Nearing high school, he became interested in the ancient mythologies, old cultures, and world histories upon which many of the stories he read or watched were actually based. These interests led him to a degree in English and a minor in history from New Starkham College. After graduation, he spent a year traveling the world. He saw pyramids in Egypt, castles in Ireland, canals in Venice, Aztec ruins in Mexico, glaciers in Alaska, and volcanoes in Hawaii. He thought these sights might inspire him to write—but for some reason, his ideas never solidified into anything more than a glorified diary.

As Maggie began to read her section aloud, Eddie stared at the wavy pattern of the wood grain on the surface of the library table. Listening to the hypnotic sound of her voice, he imagined Nathaniel's story in his head. After a moment, he felt like he was actually there with him.

Finally, my journey brought me to the Carpathian Mountains of Romania. I stayed with a college friend who was doing research at the university in Bucharest. One day, while seeking a particular antiques shop specializing in vampire protection artifacts, I wandered down an alley and became lost. After walking the labyrinthine byways for nearly an hour, I came upon an old woman selling trinkets out of the doorway behind her house. On a crate, she had set up a small display of what looked like homemade jewelry. I didn't speak her language, but I understood that she wanted me to buy something. I had budgeted only enough for my exploration of the absent vampire antiques shop, so I tried to refuse her hustle, but she was insistent that I inspect one artifact in particular. She grabbed my hand, pressing a piece of metal into my palm. Attached to a sparkling chain, it was long and silver, about six inches in length, featherlight, and perpetually cold to the touch. Its body was flat and wavy like a wriggling snake. One end was wide and straight like a spoon or small shovel. The other end came to a sharp point like a pen.

I had no idea what it was, but as soon as I held it, I felt I needed to own it. I took out my wallet, but she pushed my money away, shaking her head. She said something to me that I couldn't understand, then turned around and walked through her darkened doorway, leaving me alone in the alley.

As Eddie listened, he realized that a shape had appeared in the library table's wood grain. The swirling and swooping lines of intermittent blond and brown wood looked like a face staring up at him. Long dark hair seemed to stretch toward the edge of the table, framing an uneven, lighter patch of wood from which empty eye sockets glared, skull-like, above a thin, angry mouth. Eddie's heart raced as he stopped hearing what Maggie was reading.

The face appeared to be moving. For a moment, it seemed to smile. Then it parted its lips as Eddie pushed himself quickly away from the table. He gasped and said, "Do you guys see—"

"Excuse me." Mr. Lyons, the school librarian, emerged

from behind a bookshelf. "Where are you kids supposed to be this period?" he said.

Eddie nearly screamed. When he glanced at the table again, the face had disappeared. Had it only been his imagination? He stared at the table in disbelief. It took him a few seconds to realize that they had been caught. Mr. Lyons stood in the nearby aisle with his hands shoved into his pockets. The three kids glanced at each other, as if trying to psychically communicate before returning to the librarian.

"Well?" said Mr. Lyons.

"We're working on a project," said Harris. "For . . . uh . . . extra credit."

"Ah," said Mr. Lyons. "The infamous extra-credit excuse . . ." He approached their table, planted his fists on the surface, and leaned over the notebook in which Harris had been scribbling. Eddie worried that Mr. Lyons would ask what they were doing and then confiscate all of their work, but he didn't seem to notice the strange words on the pages of *The Enigmatic Manuscript.*

"Get back to class now, and I won't report you," said Mr. Lyons. "However, if you're caught in the hallway without a pass, don't come crying to me. I will deny this conversation ever happened." He flashed them a peace symbol, turned around, and walked away.

The kids stared at each other, then burst into nervous laughter. Eddie quickly glanced at the table again, to see if the face in the wood grain had returned. If the face had been there at all, Mr. Lyons seemed to have frightened it away. Eddie covered his own face, hoping silently that he was not going nuts.

"What do we do now?" said Harris. "There's so much left to translate."

"I'm pretty sure Mr. Lyons won't let us use the photocopier now, so we can't split the code up like we did today. Only one of us can keep working on the book tonight," Maggie answered, pushing her chair from the table and standing up. "Later we can meet up and read it all together. Maybe tomorrow?"

"Good idea," said Eddie quietly. "But who should keep translating it?"

Harris and Maggie glanced at each other. "It's your book, Eddie," said Harris. "I think you should be the one who works on it tonight . . . if you want to, that is."

Eddie nodded. "I'll keep my eyes open for anything important," he said. Distracted by the memory of the wood-grain face, he gathered *The Enigmatic Manuscript,* their translation, and the piece of paper on which Maggie had written the code key, and shoved everything in his book bag. Translating the book by himself was a daunting task, but he knew he could do it. He only needed to stay focused.

As they made their way to the front of the library, Eddie wondered if he should mention the face to Harris and Maggie. But before he had a chance, the bell rang, startling him. He jumped.

"Call me tonight if you figure anything out. Good luck!" said Harris, pushing open the library door and disappearing with Maggie.

14

When Eddie came home from school, his mother was sitting at the kitchen table, typing on her laptop computer. She was transcribing from a notebook, which was sitting on the table. She was so intent on the computer screen that she didn't glance up at Eddie as he said hello. When he tapped her on the shoulder, she nearly fell out of her chair.

"Edgar!" she said, finally seeing him standing next to her. "You scared me!" She took a deep breath and flipped the notebook over. Then she closed the computer. "I'm sorry. I'm coming up to the scariest chapter of my story. I've been sitting here, frightening myself as I go along. Every little noise I hear makes me jump."

"Sounds really scary," said Eddie, wandering to the counter and grabbing an apple. "When can I see it?"

"I'll be done within the next couple days, I think," she

said. She tapped her fingernails on the table. She seemed distracted. "I saw a sign for an open-mic night on Saturday, at the bookstore in town. The Enigmatic Manuscript, I think it's called?"

"That's Harris's mother's store," said Eddie.

"I know. I'm considering reading a chapter or two. Will you come watch? I think you'll like it."

"Of course," said Eddie, nodding as he took a bite of the apple. "I'm sure Harris will like it too."

After a moment, she cleared her throat. "And on a more serious note, I received a phone call from school today."

"Really?" said Eddie, forcing himself to smile blankly. "About what?"

"They said you cut your history and English classes. Is that true?"

Eddie steadied himself by leaning against the counter near the kitchen sink. He nodded.

"I thought you loved those subjects," she said. "What's going on?"

He didn't know how to explain himself. *Everything's fine, Mom. Except that Nathaniel Olmstead believed that he'd done something to open some sort of gate, and now, for some reason, Gatesweed is filled with monsters.*

"Edgar," she said, "I'm very happy that you've been making friends here in Gatesweed, but if these kids are talking you into . . ." She paused, then shook her head. "Well, I hope you'll use better judgment next time."

"It won't happen again," he whispered.

"That's for sure," said Mom, opening her computer. "No television for the rest of the week."

"Okay," he said, trying to sound disappointed.

As soon as Eddie finished his snack, he brought his book bag upstairs and closed his bedroom door. He took out *The Enigmatic Manuscript*, *The Wish of the Woman in Black*, Maggie's code key, and the notebook pages of their translations. He laid everything on his bed, turned on his lamp, and propped three pillows against his headboard. Leaning against them, he settled back and opened his own notebook. For a brief moment, the wood-grain face from the library table flashed before his eyes, but then he noticed Maggie's handwriting meandering across the notebook page. He forced the strange image out of his head and began to read.

I took out my wallet, but she pushed my money away, shaking her head. She said something to me that I couldn't understand, then turned around and walked through her darkened doorway, leaving me alone in the alley.

Chewing on the end of his pen, Eddie scanned the page several times before he finally opened *The Enigmatic Manuscript* to where they'd been when Mr. Lyons had appeared. What was going to happen? Would tonight be the night he finally learned Nathaniel Olmstead's fate? Or would the story end as abruptly as the book about the Woman in Black?

Finally, Eddie started to translate. He worked through each paragraph, transcribing every letter, leaving behind big bunches of words, which he then went back and read every few pages. He found it easier to understand that way.

Nathaniel Olmstead showed the Romanian woman's strange metal object to his friend, who was impressed. Being a student of antiquity, his friend assured him that the object was not Romanian and most definitely had nothing to do with vampires. He showed Nathaniel an article from a history textbook about the legend of an enigmatic "key," which some people believed had once locked the gates of Eden.

"Are you suggesting that this is the same 'key'?" I asked my friend incredulously. "That I own the 'key' to the gates of Eden?"

"A fake, of course," my friend told me, amused. "A replica. According to the descriptions I've read in several other texts, yours certainly fits the legend. What a strange souvenir!"

At the time, I was not sure what I believed. According to the article my friend had provided, academics were interested in the stories people invented in order to make sense of their lives. This I understood. The myth of the Garden of Eden, the theory of the Big Bang, every single "once upon a time" you ever heard when your parents tucked you into bed—these help us imagine our own personal world. And wasn't that the job of the writer? To create worlds? To invent myths? I'd finally found a topic about which I was excited. I was so interested in these theories that I studied as much as I could about my mysterious souvenir "key." One day, I found a comprehensive article about "the real thing" in a book called The Myth of the Stone Children.

As Eddie read what he'd translated, he gasped. *The Myth of the Stone Children*? He thought of the statue in the Nameless Woods—she was a "stone child," wasn't she? Did the statue have something to do with Nathaniel's experience in Europe? Finally, something was starting to make sense!

Glancing outside, Eddie noticed the sky quickly fading to night. Many of the leaves had fallen from the trees, so the bare branches were left in silhouette against the deep blue. They looked like bones clawing up from the earth. He licked his lips and got back to work.

The central mythology of the stone children was similar to many of the Judeo-Christian beliefs Nathaniel was familiar with—but there were also quite a few differences. According to the text he had found, some people believed that God created the world in seven days. When He was done, there existed a place called Eden—an enormous garden surrounded by a tall circular wall that protected the paradise from the yet unforged, darker realms. On either side of an ornate entrance stood two statues. Two stone children. One boy and one girl. The pedestals on which the children perched were intricately decorated with signs and symbols of the creatures who were to be kept out of paradise. Each child held a large blank book, marked by one of two Hebrew letters carved onto its cover—*Yod* on one book; *Chet* on the other.

Together the letters spelled the Hebrew word *Chai,* which roughly translated to the English word *life.*

"Maggie was right," said Eddie aloud. Then the weight of his realization descended upon him. A stone child. Holding a large blank book. Marked by one of the Hebrew letters: *Chet. Life, inside these walls . . .* Was that what the symbols meant? Eddie wondered.

If Life was contained *inside,* then what had God left *outside* of the Garden? Was *The Enigmatic Manuscript* implying what he thought?

Eddie continued to read.

The gate where the stone children stood was guarded by an archangel whose job was to act as the Voice of God. He held the key to the Garden and watched it carefully. Whenever any creature was refused passage into the Garden, the archangel used the key to carve its image into the stone pedestals as a record of its depravity. The symbols illustrating the stone gate served as a reminder of which creatures were doomed to exile.

Eddie looked up, his heart thumping, his mouth dry. He put down the book and stood up. His head was spinning. He wanted to call Harris and tell him about everything he'd just read. The statue in the woods . . . she *must* be one of these stone children! The thought seemed incredible, but then again, so did everything that had happened to him in the past month. All the secrets, the codes, and especially the monsters, seemed like impossibilities from one of Nathaniel's stories, but Eddie now knew they were not fiction.

Compelled by curiosity, Eddie continued to read.

Beyond the stone children at the gate, inside the Garden, God had created the first man and woman. Throughout history, most people have understood these to be Adam and Eve, but according to *The Myth of the Stone Children,* Eve was not the first woman. Before Eve ever existed, Adam had a wife named Lilith. Unlike Eve, Lilith did not come from a piece of his rib. Lilith was Adam's other half, his equal. She and Adam lived together in Eden for quite some time. Like every married couple, they fought. One day, they fought so terribly that God came and asked them what was wrong. In haste, Adam answered that Lilith had wronged him and should be punished. God took him at his word and banished Lilith from the Garden. He sent her far away, to a place where the Garden's light did not reach.

Lilith's only companions in her new home were the Exiled—the most vile, wretched creatures in their world.

Lilith's children were their children. These children became known as the Lilim; they too were Exiles.

According to the legend Nathaniel had found, after the infamous incident with the serpent and the tree of knowledge, God smashed Eden's wall into thousands of pieces and scattered them far across the globe. Where the pieces fell, the fabric of our world became weak. Sometimes the fabric was so thin, people could see through it into darker realms bordering our own. Having traveled to these places for inspiration, for advice, and for prayer, humans learned the sites of the fallen wall were sacred, but also dangerous. When glancing into other worlds, they never knew who might be glancing back. According to *The Myth of the Stone Children,* Lilith's children were tired of living in darkness. Some wanted to live in the light of our world. Others only wanted to destroy it. The Lilim were unsatisfied looking through the veil. They wanted more. They wanted a door.

As he studied, Nathaniel learned that several hundred years ago, a scholar familiar with the mythology discovered a strange instrument, which he believed was the archangel's key. The instrument was a necklace from which dangled a sharp silver pendant. From his studies, he concluded that this key could lead whoever possessed it to the places where the walls of Eden had tumbled. It was also the scholar's opinion that this instrument, if used correctly, had the power to puncture a hole in the fabric between the worlds.

The lamp on Eddie's bedside table flickered and dimmed. He dropped his pen with a shout. "What the heck?" Eddie whispered to himself, scrambling to the center of the mattress in case he was suddenly thrown into darkness. He turned and stared at the lamp for a few seconds. The light remained defiantly faint.

For a moment, he tried to convince his wild imagination that it was a perfectly normal occurrence, a power surge of some sort, but after the creepy experiences of the past few days, he understood quickly that it might be something less ordinary. It was not a pleasant thought.

He imagined a sharp-clawed hand, reaching up from the side of the bed, tugging on his quilt. *"Stop it,"* he whispered, smacking his forehead with the palm of his hand. He then called "Mom!" toward his closed bedroom door. He waited for several quiet seconds, but she did not answer. "Dad!" he tried, but he was met again only by the subtle creaking of the house as the breeze came up the hill.

Where are they? he thought. He looked at the clock, wondering if they might be asleep. It flashed twelve o'clock repeatedly. Maybe there had been an electrical shortage, after all.

Eddie realized he had no idea how long he'd been

working. He pulled aside his curtain and peeked out the window. Gatesweed was quiet at the bottom of the hill—most of the lights in the few inhabited houses were out. It must be later than he thought.

As he was about to shut the curtain, Eddie noticed something strange happening in the center of town. It started with the park lights in the town green suddenly, collectively hushing out. Eddie watched as the streetlights on Center Street blinked out too. With each passing second, another circle of streetlights turned off. Then the buildings in between each concentric street seemed to lose power as well. Eddie had never seen anything like this before—during a normal power outage, all the electricity went out at once. But the darkness at the bottom of the hill seemed to be creeping toward him, like a disease.

The light on his bedside table dimmed even further, and Eddie groaned.

Unable to control himself, he leapt into the middle of his bedroom floor, clearing at least an arm's length between where he landed and the dark space under his bed. Then he raced toward his bedroom door and yanked it open. The pitch-dark upstairs hallway stretched before him. Eddie paused and turned around. The thing with claws he imagined waiting for him underneath his mattress might still be there, but Eddie did not yet run. The darkness in the hallway seemed just as threatening.

As he stood in his doorway contemplating whether or not to peer under his bed, the light on his nightstand simply sputtered out. Darkness weighed upon the house like a musty quilt. Eddie's throat felt like it was closing up, but he managed to call down the hallway for his parents. Again, they seemed not to hear him; he didn't receive an answer. Eddie wondered if they were even in the house at all. Where else would they be at such a late hour?

Eddie began to feel claustrophobic. He could barely see—the hallway was more like a vague impression than the real thing. He stepped farther into the hallway, clutched at the cold glass doorknob, and swung the door shut.

Searching for the nearest light switch, he swiped at the wall. He found it, but when he flicked the switch, nothing happened. Eddie exhaled slowly, trying to compose himself. Next, he took a purposeful step toward his parents' bedroom. Keeping his eyes straight forward, Eddie managed to make his way there. While terrified by the silence filling the house, he was also thankful that nothing was growling, whispering, or scratching from inside the walls—as so often happened in Nathaniel Olmstead's books during moments like this.

He knocked at his parents' bedroom door but didn't wait for a response before turning the knob and swinging the door open. "Hello?" he said, stepping forward into the room. He heard the sheets rustling. Thank goodness, Eddie thought, scrambling quickly across the floor to his mother's side of the bed. "It must be later than I thought," he said quietly.

He reached out to touch her. He knew she wouldn't mind him waking her—he'd done it before when he'd had a nightmare. He could feel her shoulder underneath the down comforter, but she didn't respond, not even when he shook her slightly. "Mom!" he whispered.

Finally, she groaned in her sleep, then mumbled something. It sounded like, "What's the matter?"

Eddie thought about how to respond without sounding paranoid. Any rational person could explain away his fears within seconds. *The power's gone out. Go back to bed.* But Eddie didn't want to go back to bed by himself—not after everything he'd learned from reading *The Enigmatic Manuscript.*

There was nearly a half-foot of space at the edge of the bed, so Eddie lay there, on top of the blanket. I'll just stay until the power comes back on, he thought.

He smelled his mother's fruity shampoo, but quickly the scent changed. It was no longer sweet, like his mother, but it was horrible—vaguely familiar, like something he'd experienced in a nightmare. He remembered the odor from Nathaniel Olmstead's basement, when he and Harris had been reading *The Wish of the Woman in Black.* Where was it coming from? Eddie sat up, holding his nose. He listened to his parents' breathing beside him. Sleeping soundly, they seemed not to notice the stench.

Eddie couldn't stomach it; the smell was making him sick.

Reaching out toward his mother, he touched what he thought was her hair sprawled across the pillow. But the feel of it was unlike his mother's long curls. His fingers clutched at what felt like cobwebs—thin, sticky strands that clung to his hand as he pulled away in horror. "Mom!" Eddie screamed. But instead of sitting up suddenly, his parents continued to lie in bed. His father even started to snore. "Wake up!" he said. He drew his hand away, as what he thought had been his mother finally turned over to look at him.

It was a shape blacker than the shadows that rose from the bed and towered over Eddie, who continued to lie on the mattress frozen in terror.

He knew who she was. Impossible as it seemed, he'd seen her staring at him from the wood grains in the library table that afternoon. Eddie thought he might puke.

Her weathered face, so white it was almost green, hovered near the ceiling and glimmered in the darkness like an alien moon. Her skin was chapped, transparent, like wet paper. Her tattered, malignant hair hung from her head like rotting seaweed—long, ragged, and blacker than the deepest part of the ocean. Her eyes were dark empty holes, and her lipless mouth gaped like a fish. Heavy black robes stretched away from her body like shadows being pulled away from the walls. As she moved forward, she clenched her hands in front of herself. Her face tightened as she seemed to squint at him.

Eddie wiped a tickle at the back of his collar. Sweat.

Wake up, she said in a mimicking, high-pitched voice. *Wake up,* she repeated. *Wake up.* Then she started to laugh—a dark din totally unlike the voice she'd just used to taunt him. The sound hurt his ears. Her robes lifted and swirled around her as she reached toward him. The woman's hair whipped at her face. Her black eyes expanded until they were all he knew.

He was falling into them. He couldn't stop. There was nothing to hold on to. Nothing but darkness and the sound of laughter and the rush of—

Thump!

Eddie fell off the bed and hit the ground. He scrambled backward and toppled his mother's bedside table. Her lamp turned over and crashed to the floor. Eddie leapt to his feet, suddenly furious. "What did you do with my parents?" he shouted at the woman, remembering the book in which Dylan finds two soggy piles of pajamas on the living room floor. If he stuck around for much longer, he knew he'd end up just like that. She reached toward him, but Eddie ducked. He managed to run to the end of the bed and around the corner of the bedpost, where he had a straight shot for the door. But halfway across the room, he slipped on the rug. As he struggled to stand, he felt a chill run up his spine. The Woman stood inches behind him, her face nearly a foot over his own. Before he had a chance to scream, she seemed to smile. A horrible, humorless, manipulative smile, but a smile nonetheless.

Eddie . . ., her voice purred—deeply, vibrantly. It reminded him of the soft string-quartet music his parents sometimes played on the stereo during dinner. *Why do you want to hurt me?*

"I . . . I *don't* want to hurt you," he heard himself say. He looked at his hands; for some reason, he wasn't melting.

Good boy . . ., she continued. *Stay away from things which do not concern you. . . . Put that book back on the shelf. . . .* Her hair reminded him of plant tendrils floating in underwater currents. *Read something else instead,* she continued. *Something . . . happier. Prettier. Less . . . frightening.*

Eddie didn't know what to say. "I . . . I . . . ," was all that came out of his mouth when he tried to speak.

Unless you like being frightened . . ., she whispered. *Do you?* Her eye sockets widened. She waited for his answer, as if she were truly curious, or almost amused. *Do you like being scared, Eddie? Because scary is something I am quite good at. . . . I have had many years of experience. . . .*

Her face was no longer a face. It was a long hallway in a secret, underground place through which he found himself hurtling, his feet skidding against the slick, dark floor. At the end of the hallway, twenty feet away, a swarm of black insects so dense it seemed to fold in upon itself beckoned to him like a hand. He reached for the walls, trying to find something to hold on to, but his fingers kept slipping against the wet stone. He clenched his mouth shut, trying to keep his screams in and the insects out.

Eddie turned and to his surprise found he was still standing in his parents' bedroom. He grabbed at the doorknob, wrenching it open and running blindly into the hallway. When he reached the top of the stairs, he grabbed the handrail and swung himself around the corner. Taking three steps at a time, he leapt down the staircase, until he missed one and slid the rest of the way to the rug in the foyer.

Someone clutched at his shoulders, shaking him.

His father was leaning over him. "Edgar! Are you okay?"

Eddie glanced around, unsure of where he was or what was happening. As he tried to sit up at the bottom of the stairs, a dull pain throbbed in his tailbone. He groaned.

"What's wrong?" asked Mom. Eddie turned to find her peering up from her place at the kitchen table. She appeared to still be writing, as if she hadn't moved since Eddie had come home from school.

"He fell down the stairs," said Dad. "I saw the whole thing from the couch in the living room."

Eddie stood up. His parents both seemed so calm. He nearly grabbed his father to give him a hug but stopped himself. He didn't want to alarm them by being upset. "When did the power come back on?" said Eddie evenly. He held on to the banister at the bottom of the stairs to keep his hands from shaking. His parents were looking at him funny.

"The power's been on all night," said Dad. He felt Eddie's forehead with the back of his hand. "Are you sure you're okay?"

Eddie wasn't sure of the answer to that question. He turned around and looked up the stairs. He could see the light spilling from his bedroom. "But the lights were . . ." Eddie peered out the window next to the front door. The entire town was lit up as usual. Had the whole thing been a dream? Impossible. Eddie was certain that he'd been awake the whole time. He'd been too excited by Nathaniel's story to fall asleep. "What—what time is it?" he said.

"Nearly midnight," said Mom. "We thought you were asleep upstairs."

"You mean you've been down here the entire time? But I thought you were . . . I thought you were . . ." Eddie tried to speak, but he realized he didn't want to finish his sentence.

Plus, at this point, he wasn't sure *what* he had been thinking.

15

Eddie was late for school the next morning.

In class, Ms. Phelps called on him for the third time in twenty minutes, and he had to admit, once again, he didn't know the answer. He hadn't done any of the homework. He didn't blame Ms. Phelps for being upset—how could she possibly know that last night he had been haunted by a malicious spirit who once upon a time might have been banished from the Garden of Eden, and who might have been responsible for the disappearance of Nathaniel Olmstead? Of course, he didn't try to explain this. He knew she wouldn't understand. He would save his explanations until he met up with Harris and Maggie during lunch.

After class, Eddie found them sitting near the windows in the far corner of the cafeteria. He was late because he'd wanted to make photocopies of his translation so they could read it themselves. He'd convinced Mr. Lyons to help him by volunteering to reshelf books next week—if he was still alive. . . .

Neither Harris nor Maggie looked like they had slept much, but when they saw him approaching, they perked up. He knew they'd be excited to hear about his translation, but he didn't know how to explain everything else that had happened.

After falling down the stairs, Eddie refused to sleep in his own bedroom. Even shoved between his parents, Eddie's mind had churned with frightening images all night long. He hadn't slept either.

He slumped into the chair next to Harris and across from Maggie.

"So?" said Harris, taking a bite of his peanut butter sandwich. "How did it go? Do you know what happened to Nathaniel Olmstead?"

Eddie shook his head. "I didn't finish."

"Didn't finish?" said Maggie. "Why not?"

Eddie took a deep breath and told them everything that had happened, starting with the face he saw in the library table yesterday afternoon and ending with his horrifying encounter with the Woman. After Eddie finished his story, Harris slumped over onto the cafeteria table and threw his arms over his head.

"What's wrong?" said Maggie.

"Don't you get it?" said Harris, turning his head slightly to speak. "The legend of the woman in the woods? Like all the other monsters that have attacked us for whatever reason—touching the water at the lake, picking the flower, going into the woods at night—now *she's* coming for Eddie. She followed him down from the statue in the Nameless Woods, and she'll haunt him until he's totally gone bonkers!"

"Stop scaring him." Maggie slapped Harris's shoulder and rolled her eyes before looking at Eddie. "You're not going bonkers," she said. "She came to you for a specific reason. She doesn't want to drive you crazy. She wants *you* to leave *her* alone." She paused, thinking. "Didn't you say she told you to read something *less frightening*? Maybe she was trying to scare you so you'd stop reading *The Enigmatic Manuscript*."

Eddie bit at his bottom lip. "Should we stop? I mean . . . now that we've read about what she can do to people in *The Wish of the Woman in Black* . . . it seems really stupid to keep going."

Harris sat up. "We can't just stop! Not now that we're so close to finding out what happened to Nathaniel Olmstead. He obviously did something that made her mad. If he's in trouble . . . maybe we can help him."

"Why?" said Maggie.

The boys looked at her like she was crazy.

"He said it himself," she continued. "The creatures came through the door—whatever door he's talking about, I don't know—but he said it's *his fault.* Maybe he doesn't deserve our help."

As he sat at the lunch table, images of the Woman in Black flashed through Eddie's memory and he shuddered. But maybe Maggie was right. He pulled his book bag onto his lap. "There's so much more to the story now that you won't understand until you actually read it for yourselves." He took out the two photocopied packets he'd made for Harris and Maggie. "You'll have to tell me what you think." He handed one to each of them. "Try to read it all if you can," he said. "We'll meet at the end of the day and keep working."

After school, they quietly walked to Harris's house together. Both Harris and Maggie had managed to finish reading everything Eddie had written. Despite the Woman's threat, they were intrigued and seemed excited to find the answers to Nathaniel Olmstead's mystery. They all agreed: they might as well *try* to read a little bit more.

At the bookstore, they found Frances standing on the front porch, looking at the wooden deck beneath her feet.

"What's the matter, Mom?" said Harris, stopping at the bottom of the steps.

When Frances turned around, Eddie could see that her cheeks were blotchy red. She'd been crying. Embarrassed, she quickly wiped her face. "Oh, Harris," she said, "you brought friends." She came to the top step, reached out, and held on to the balustrades on either side of the stairs. When Harris tried to peer around her, she moved, as if trying to block his view. "Wait," she whispered.

"What the heck!" said Harris, rushing up the steps and pushing past her. She stepped aside. Eddie could see what she'd been trying to hide. Someone had spray-painted black graffiti on the floor of the porch.

The Woman Is Coming for You. . . .

Frances covered the graffiti with an old rug. She told them she would be busy with several book orders upstairs, so they had the place to themselves. Since the bookstore was empty, they organized themselves at a quiet table in the back.

Eddie felt like the graffiti had been his fault. If he hadn't picked the flower, the gremlin wouldn't have attacked them. If the gremlin hadn't attacked them, no one would have spread any rumors, and the vandals wouldn't have targeted Harris's store again.

Harris told him to forget about it. "It's happened before," he said. "It'll happen again. Besides, it can be painted over."

Looking at his friends, Eddie wondered if they weren't *all* the class freaks now. At least they would be freaks together. *The Exiled.* In a twisted way, the three of them were like the Lilim now, weren't they? Eddie kept the thought to himself.

They picked up their notebooks and pens. Eddie opened *The Enigmatic Manuscript* to the spot where he had been interrupted the night before. He laid *The Wish of the Woman in Black* open to its last page, where the code key was written. "We work together, like yesterday," he said, more determined than ever.

After researching the legend of the key in Romania for nearly a month, Nathaniel finally returned to the United States. He felt ready to be home.

Once there, he started to dream about a small town nestled in a group of wooded hills. It was called Gatesweed. The image of the town was so beautiful, he felt compelled to look up the name, to see if, somehow, the place might truly exist. To his surprise, after searching an atlas in the local library, he located a town called Gatesweed that happened to be a two-hour drive southwest of Coven's Corner. Having already traveled so far for inspiration's sake, he thought that one more jaunt—for curiosity's sake—couldn't hurt.

When Nathaniel arrived in Gatesweed, he felt like he'd come home. The hills, the mills, the park, the shape of the town itself were all familiar. Something told him to stay. With a loan from his parents, Nathaniel bought a house in the hills outside the center of the town. The place had been abandoned for years and needed plenty of work, so the price was right.

As he worked on the house during the day, he was struck by the number of story ideas that began to come to him.

With every board he tore up and every stone he replaced, another image seemed to pop into his brain. He wrote them down in his notebooks, trying to capture them before they got away.

In the midst of renovations, Nathaniel discovered a passageway in the fireplace that led to a series of catacombs under the house. He was frightened, yet intrigued, to explore the space. After several hours, he decided that it would be perfect for a private office. What better place to write creepy stories than in a secret room in the basement?

At night, Nathaniel continued to have strange dreams. Now, instead of dreaming about Gatesweed, he began to dream about the woods beyond the orchard. Just like his earlier compulsion to find Gatesweed, Nathaniel now felt the need to explore this new pastoral domain at the bottom of the hill behind his house.

The next day, I trudged over the small ridge and down into a wide, wooded flatland. I walked for almost ten minutes before coming upon a dirt clearing.

On the other side of the clearing, I could see a strange white figure staring at me—a statue of a pretty young girl. Her face was pure white, but it was her eyes that caught my attention. Something about her gave me the chills. She held a book out to me. On the spine was carved a peculiar symbol—like some sort of Hebrew letter. I was shocked. Was this the letter, Chet, I'd read about in Romania? Looking closer, I noticed images of strange creatures carved into the base on which she stood. My suspicions began to materialize, like ghosts all around me.

I thought I heard a faint voice speaking unintelligible words into my ear; I dismissed it as a figment of my imagination. But the longer I watched the statue, the more I understood. Strange knowledge washed across my brain. I was standing on the brink of something huge. The evidence was unmistakable. The statue, the book in her hands, the symbol carved onto its cover, the images of the creatures dancing on the half-buried pedestal under the child's bare feet. The words "oracle, henge, and monolith" repeated through my mind. These places truly existed—just like I'd read in The Myth of the Stone Children. And yet, reason would not allow me to believe that I had found a piece of the Garden's wall.

Certainly, this was a powerful place. Its energy was palpable. But there must be some sort of explanation, I thought. I was certain that if I stood there long enough, the answer would come to me.

I remembered the silver pendant the Romanian woman had given me. According to the texts I read, the archangel's key had the ability to lead whoever possessed it to the places where Eden's wall fell. Was it possible that the same thing had happened to me? If so, then my friend at the university had been wrong—the relic was not a fake. The pendant I had brought home was no mere souvenir. Looking into the stone child's eyes, I knew that the key, which had once unlocked the Garden of Eden's gate, was buried at the bottom of my sock drawer! The girl seemed to speak to me without words. The longer I stared at the statue, the more I felt I knew what I needed to do.

I walked all the way home, went upstairs to my bedroom, and removed the silver necklace from the drawer. It seemed to pulse in my hand with a cold heat. I was instantly filled with a great purpose. I knew then that the moment I had found this object, my destiny had been to come to Gatesweed and discover the statue in the woods—but there was something else, one final action I felt compelled to take.

I turned to a blank page in a notebook on my desk. Instinctively, I pressed the tip of the pendant to my notebook's paper. To my surprise, a black line appeared like a pen mark. Then, for a reason I could not name, I drew the symbol that was carved into the stone child's book.

Looking back, I now realize that at that moment, I had begun to tear a dangerous hole in the delicate fabric that protects our world from the mysterious ones that border it. I'd do anything now to take it all back.

"This is crazy," said Eddie.

"Do you think he's telling the truth?" said Maggie. "What if this is all just fiction?"

"After everything we've seen recently?" said Harris. "I think we can assume that he's telling the truth."

It had finally gotten dark out. Maggie cleared her throat and started rubbing her eyes. On the other side of the park, a car honked its horn. It was the first time since they'd opened the book that afternoon that they heard proof of the world outside their own private circle.

"Do you want some water?" Harris asked Maggie, who had been reading the last section aloud.

"No. I'm fine," she said. "I actually feel like I don't even really need the piece of paper to translate anymore."

"What do you think is going to happen to him?" Eddie asked.

Harris closed his eyes, as if shutting out the inevitable conclusion.

Maggie shook her head. "I have an idea," she said, "but I don't want to spoil it." Then she began where she had left off.

Using the pendant like a pencil, Nathaniel continued to write down bits and pieces of images and ideas—dark basements, secret keys to hidden doors, statues, ghosts, and demon dogs. From these notes, a story began to materialize.

Nearly a month after finding the statue in the woods, he began writing what would become his first novel, *The Rumor of the Haunted Nunnery.* After he finished, Nathaniel typed it up to send to agents and publishers. To his surprise, one of them wanted it, and shortly thereafter, it was published. He was thrilled that people were finally reading something he'd written.

He wrote all of the books using the pendant. On the first page, he wrote the title and his name. Below these words, he drew the Hebrew symbol. On the next page, he began the tale. If someone were to ask why he wrote the books that way, he wouldn't have been able to provide a logical answer. It was something he just had to do—as if the silver pendant, or the statue in the woods, or *something* was providing unconscious instruction. But the process worked. When he used the pendant to write, he became especially inspired. He felt that if he questioned why, it might all go away, so he stopped asking questions. For a while.

As the books continued to sell, Nathaniel began to read reports in the newspapers of strange occurrences in Gatesweed. Several pets had disappeared under mysterious circumstances. A few children claimed to have seen unusual animals wandering through the woods near Nathaniel's driveway. Several people actually asserted that these animals had attacked them. A twelve-year-old boy named Jeremy Quakerly vanished from his bedroom in the middle of the night. Finally, the body of an elderly schoolteacher was found in the middle of a cornfield on one of the county roads past the mills. The incident was ruled an accident, but a rumor spread throughout Gatesweed that on the death certificate, the coroner had listed the cause of death as a fall from a great height. She had died in her bathrobe.

Nathaniel heard some people claim that these reports echoed what he had written in his stories, but he convinced himself they were coincidences. Or he attempted to, at least. Nathaniel understood that any writer has his share of critics, so he tried to ignore the cruel looks and harsh whispers that followed him in town.

He sometimes wandered through the woods behind the apple orchard, exploring the clearing where the mysterious statue stood. There, he contemplated his fortune. Was there validity to the rumors? What was he actually doing when he used the pen to write his stories? Was the legend of the archangel's key actually true? Other than the fact that the piece of metal could write on paper, did it actually hold mystical properties like the scholars said it should? After all, a pencil could write on paper too. Nathaniel would stand at the edge of the statue's clearing and shake his head in disbelief. He told himself that this world was meant to remain mysterious. Deep down, though, he believed it was easier to choose ignorance.

Everything changed one afternoon, years later, when I wandered near the Nameless Lake. Of course, I'd seen the small body of water before, having used it as a set piece for the end of The Rumor of the Haunted Nunnery. That day, I stepped onto the pebbly shoreline, allowing my boots to send small ripples out into the water, something I hadn't done before. Some time later, several dogs leapt from the water and chased me halfway through the woods. By the time I'd made it home, my mind was racing. I couldn't fathom what I'd seen. All the reports I'd read in the newspapers, all the unsolved crimes I'd dismissed as coincidence—the missing pets, the strange wild animal attacks, the child's disappearance from his bedroom, the schoolteacher's death—came flooding back. People in Gatesweed had whispered for years that I was responsible for the odd happenings around town. Now I'd seen it with my own eyes. Apparently, at least, my monster lake-dogs were real.

How could that be? All my doubts about the pendant were suddenly half erased. If the legend of the key was real, was it possible that using the pendant to write my books had somehow made the dogs appear in the woods behind my house? Was it possible that some of the other monsters from my books were real too? If the stone child supposedly marked a place where the fabric between the worlds is thin, maybe I had caused the fabric to rip? If that was true, was I responsible for everything that had happened?

I immediately went and hid the pendant in my basement. I needed to get away from it for a while, stop writing, take a break and think about everything.

Several days later, I was lying on my couch for an afternoon nap when I heard a noise that sounded like papers being shuffled. I realized that something was standing in the doorway to my kitchen. At first, I thought it was something in my eye, a piece of dust or an eyelash, but when I rubbed there, nothing happened. A dark patch filled the space where there should have been a stove and a sinkful of dirty dishes. I sat up as the dark patch took form. It was an old woman. Shadows swirled around her body like smoke. Her hair lapped at her face in waves as if a slight breeze blew through my house. Her mouth did not move, but I heard her voice clearly. It was old and reminded me of dust.

The Woman touched the door frame in which she stood. The door grew and the kitchen behind it disappeared into the flickering glow of an unseen fire. This place was no longer my house. I heard wings flapping and insects scuttling through the shadows. The walls grew dark and dripped with moisture.

The Woman's eye sockets were black holes, but they focused on me intently.

"Who are you?" I asked. She didn't answer me, but somehow I knew her. "Lilith?" I whispered. She smiled but said nothing to confirm my suspicion. Still, I understood what she wanted from me. She wished for me to release her—like I had released her children, I realized now.

"If I write you into a story, will you exist here, like the dogs that chased me through the woods?" I stumbled in my thoughts, afraid of the answer to my question. I remembered the reports of the unsolved crimes. I was terrified by the possibility of my own unwitting guilt. "Like—like the others I wrote about?"

She showed me the statue in the dark woods. The stone child glimmered, filling the clearing with cold blue radiance. In a burst of light, a pack of dogs surrounded the statue. With their eyes glowing red, the dogs dashed into the shadows. All at once, I saw images of other monsters manifesting in the clearing beside the illuminated girl. I now understood completely how the portal worked. As I finished each story, the statue glowed, the gate opened, and the creatures emerged.

The Woman spoke. "The key plays games with me." Her dark voice jabbed into my chest, like a needle and thread. "Lost and found. Years passed. It brought you here to me. You have written the stories of my children. Now that they have all come through the gate in the woods, it is time for you to begin another story . . . mine."

"And if I don't?" I dared to speak.

The woman's face changed—in it I saw myself locked in a dark room, water rising from the floor below; I saw myself in the middle of a haunted city, pale faces staring at me through grease-smudged storefronts; I saw myself falling into a pit as wide as the ocean and blacker than night, from which rose the steady screaming of a million tortured souls. The Woman reached out to me and laughed, her voice rising like a flurry of ravens swirling into a dark, dead sky.

I woke up on my couch. Sweating. My chest hurt. I was breathing hard, and my legs felt heavy. The Woman was gone. My house looked the same as always. I wondered what had just happened. Had I been dreaming? Was I going crazy?

I sat on the couch and contemplated my predicament. If I didn't listen to her, would she haunt me forever with such visions? If what I had seen was not a dream, as the evidence overwhelmingly suggested, then I was, in fact, guilty for releasing the monsters, the legendary Lilim, one at a time from their purgatorial prisons. Simply holding the pendant had equipped me with the unconscious knowledge of how to use it. I was certain now that the pendant had brought me to Gatesweed in the first place. When I used the pendant to write my stories, it acted like a key. Each story had opened a door in the woods, where the stone child held her empty book, like she had when she stood beside Eden's gate. This new door led to places where the monsters were real. No wonder the

"You know what?" said Harris. "I sort of hope so. Because if some*one* is back there, that means that some*thing* isn't."

"Maybe it's nothing," said Eddie. "Sometimes in old buildings, lights flicker by themselves. Right?"

"Right," said Harris and Maggie, sounding too enthusiastic, as if they were trying to convince themselves.

"But maybe we should finish reading the book somewhere else?" said Maggie.

The lights fluttered again, briefly. Eddie remembered what had happened in his bedroom the night before. He shuttled his chair closer to Maggie. He didn't want to finish reading the book at all.

"I think that's a good idea. Let's go upstairs," said Harris, sliding his chair back and standing up.

The lights in the back of the store suddenly went out. The only lights on now were the two table lamps near the front door.

Eddie knocked his own chair backward as he stood. It banged against the hardwood floor, sending shivers across his skin. Then he saw Maggie's face as she stared toward the street, and his shivers became an arctic chill.

"You guys . . . ," she said, nodding toward the town green.

When Eddie turned around, he saw only his reflection in the window. "What's wrong?" he said.

old Romanian woman had wanted to get rid of the pendant! How ma cursed hands had it passed through over the years? To realize I he such power in my fingertips was more terrifying than my wor nightmare.

I thought about what I should do. I was certainly willing to p down the pendant, to stop writing, or at least try to write something with out monsters in it. I had never been able to do so before, but I w older now, with more experience. I had become a different perso Hadn't I?

However, if I refused to tell her story, would the Woman send more bad dreams? Was that the worst she could do?

At that point, I was certain I could handle it. That was before

The lights in the back of the store flickered, and M stopped reading. The three kids looked toward the door i rear wall. It was open a crack. No one said anything Eddie knew what they were all feeling. The pen in Ma hand was shaking. Harris clutched the table. Eddie started to twitch. The big bookshelf on the left side o door obscured the overhead light, so it was impossible t inside the storage room. Blackness gaped through the cra the doorway.

"Mom?" called Harris, his voice shaky.

"I thought you said she was upstairs," said Eddie.

"*Is* there someone back there?" Maggie whispered.

Eddie and Harris glanced at each other.

"The lights in the park . . . They've gone out too," said Harris.

Eddie glanced toward the back of the store. It might have been his imagination, but he thought he could see movement through the open door. He turned around, refusing to look.

"Not only the park," said Maggie, squinting, "but it looks like the whole town has gone dark."

"We need to get out of here," said Harris. He shoved *The Enigmatic Manuscript* under his arm and grabbed the notebook and pen. "Now."

Eddie nodded. He snatched his book bag and ran toward the front door. As he reached for the knob, Maggie ran up beside him and tugged on his sleeve.

"Wait," she said. "We don't know what's out there."

Suddenly, Eddie heard a familiar voice in the back of the store. *Why?* it said in a soft, singsong manner. *Eddie . . . why do you want to hurt me . . . ?*

"Do—do you guys hear that?" said Eddie.

"Hear what?" said Harris.

The two table lamps in the store began to flicker as well. Over Maggie's shoulder, Eddie saw someone moving through the shadows, reaching out toward him. His voice caught in his throat as he turned around and threw the front door open into the night. Then he ran.

As he hurtled across the front porch and down the stairs, he heard his friends behind him. They leapt from the last step onto the sidewalk, hopped over the curb, and skidded into the middle of the street.

When they turned around, they saw that the only light in the entire town spilled dimly from the windows of The Enigmatic Manuscript. All Eddie could see of the other buildings on Center Street were silent silhouettes against a starless sky.

Inside, the store now seemed empty. Those vague arms Eddie had seen reaching from the shadows were gone. Eddie glanced over his shoulder to the park.

Could she have followed them out of the store? Could she be with them out here in the dark street?

"What's happening?" said Maggie.

"I heard her talking to me," said Eddie. "She asked me why I want to hurt her."

"I thought I heard someone talking in the store too," she said. "But I figured it was my imagination."

"The Woman in Black," said Harris, crossing his arms over his chest. His voice started to rise. "She's coming for all of us now?"

"We need to stay calm," said Eddie. "We still have some light left. If we stay quiet, maybe we can sit here and—"

"Are you crazy?" said Harris. "You want to sit in the middle of the cold dark street and keep reading this stupid thing? No way! I want to find someplace nice and bright to hide."

"That's it," said Maggie quietly.

"What do you mean?" said Harris. "What's it?"

The light from the store gave Maggie's eyes a fierce glow. "She keeps asking Eddie why he wants to hurt her. But *why* does she think he's hurting her? What have we been doing for the past couple days?"

Eddie and Harris glanced at each other. "All we've been doing is reading Nathaniel Olmstead's book," said Harris.

"Right!" Maggie pointed at the book Harris had tucked under his arm. *The Enigmatic Manuscript.* "When Eddie was translating the book last night, he only got so far because she interrupted him. Just like we were interrupted right now." Maggie thought about that. "Maybe she's afraid of what we'll learn if we finish reading the book." She smiled. "That only makes me want to read it more."

The lights inside the store began to flicker again, this time dimming almost all the way out.

"We won't be able to read anything if the lights go out," said Eddie. He huddled closer to his friends.

Harris cried out, pointing toward the apartment above the store. The light turned on in the kitchen window. Frances's silhouette appeared. She raised her hands to the glass, as if trying to block the glare to see outside. Then she lifted the pane and leaned over the windowsill. She didn't seem to notice that the entire town had fallen into darkness. "Are you kids hungry?" she called to them.

"Mom!" shouted Harris. "Watch out!"

Behind Frances, another silhouette loomed. It rose and expanded, filling the bright kitchen window with shadow until the room went dark.

"Mom!" Harris cried again.

Then all the lights went out. Downstairs. Upstairs. Eddie's body stiffened as Maggie clutched at his arm. He could barely see her face.

"Mom! She's behind you!" Harris called as he started running toward the side door.

"Harris!" Maggie shouted.

"Don't go in there!" Eddie called to Harris's running silhouette. Then, before he could stop himself, he chased after his friend. Maggie followed close behind. He heard the screen door slam. Eddie followed the sound, yanking the door open. Maggie caught it from behind him. She held it open as Eddie stared up into the darkness. He could hear Harris tripping up the steps. He had to turn off his brain so that he would not imagine Harris falling into the cold arms of the looming silhouette.

"Mom! I'm coming!" Harris cried.

Despite being unable to see, Eddie took the stairs two at a time. Using the handrail, he yanked his way to the top and flung himself through the doorway.

But the overhead light in the kitchen blinded him.

Eddie found Harris in the middle of the room hugging Frances. Harris heaved sobs into his mother's neck, and

Frances glanced at Eddie, as if to say, *What are you kids up to?*

Maggie bumped into Eddie's back as she came up the stairs, pushing him forward into the kitchen. Eddie caught a glimpse out the window. The town green was lit up as usual, as were all the buildings on Center Street.

The Woman in Black was gone. It was as if she had never even been here.

"Honey, what's the matter?" said Frances, pushing Harris away so she could see his face. "This is *not* the Spanish Inquisition. I only asked if you were hungry."

Harris turned away, wiping at his eyes, embarrassed. "Are we hungry, you guys?" he said. Eddie and Maggie nodded slowly. Turning back toward his mother, Harris said, "Can they stay for dinner? We're working on a project tonight." He choked back a sob, finally composing himself. "Hopefully, we'll be done soon."

"Of course," said Frances, looking concerned. She went to the sink and turned on the faucet. Filling a saucepan with water, she glanced over her shoulder. "For goodness' sake, Harris, I had no idea you took your homework so *seriously.*"

In Harris's bedroom, they placed *The Enigmatic Manuscript* and their translations in the middle of the floor and sat in a triangle around them. They stared at the book in silence for a whole minute before Maggie said, "Whose turn is it?"

"If we keep reading, is she going to come after us again?" said Harris, still shaken. "Is she going to come after my *mom* again?"

Maggie picked at her fingernail. "She might want us to think she will. But I have a feeling that we should keep reading anyway."

"Even if she tries to . . . ," Eddie started. But he couldn't think of how to end the sentence. "Tries to . . ."

"Tries to *scare* us?" Maggie finished. "That's all she's been doing so far."

Eddie flinched. "Wait a second," he said. "You're right. All she *has* been doing is scaring us. Like her bark is worse than her bite?"

"But *barking* is not all she can do," said Harris. "You read *The Wish of the Woman in Black* yourself. She's evil."

"No. She's angry," said Maggie. "But if she's so powerful, why hasn't she turned us into little black piles of goo, like she's so good at?"

"Maggie!" Eddie said, leaning forward and clutching her arm. "She might be listening."

"So what?" said Maggie, yanking herself away. "I think if she really could stop us from reading this book, she'd have done it already, instead of performing these little parlor tricks. Flickering lights? I mean . . . are we really that scared of the dark?"

"Yes!" said Eddie and Harris at the same time.

"*This* is why I don't read these kinds of books!" said Maggie. "Being scared makes you act like an idiot."

"Hey," said Eddie, "you weren't the one she spoke to. Maybe if you'd been there last night, you'd understand. . . ."

"I'm here now," Maggie answered quietly, "and *we* need to finish reading the book." She picked it up and handed it to Eddie. She smiled and said, "We can do it. I know we can."

. . . that was before the nightmares began.

I would tumble from my bed, screaming into the night. The darkness coaxed me back to bed, but as soon as I placed my head on the pillow, the awful visions returned—children with no faces, cities full of gravestones, hands clawing at me from behind my wallpaper, shadows that tied me to the floor—and all the while, the sound of the Woman's laughter taunted me.

Finally, I stopped sleeping at all. During the day, I was a zombie. Since putting away the pendant, writing was impossible, so sometimes, I pulled it from the desk drawer in the basement, wondering if I should simply write the Woman's story. But I had promised myself I wouldn't. At that point, the thought of another missing child on my conscience was enough to deter me from using the pendant to write.

But I was certainly tempted. If I gave the Woman what she wanted, she might leave me alone. After that, I could throw the pendant away, bury it somewhere, hide it. Deep down, I knew it was not so simple.

The longer I waited, the worse the dreams became. Soon, whenever I closed my eyes, for even a few seconds, the most horrible, violent, and disgusting images flashed across the backs of my eyelids, like monster movies in a run-down movie theater. I wasn't sure how much more I could take. I had become short-tempered and irritable. I began to suspect that I was losing my mind. If I didn't do something soon, not only would my few friends in town stop wanting to be near me anymore, but I wouldn't be able to function in public at all. Everywhere I looked I imagined some new horror. What I could see most clearly was my future—locked in a padded cell.

Eddie stopped reading. In the ceiling, the light had started to flicker.

Maggie shook her head. "Keep reading, Eddie. She only wants us to stop." She looked toward the ceiling, as if the Woman was watching them from up there. "But we're not going to!" she shouted.

Shaken, Eddie slowly turned away from the overhead light and looked at the page. He steadied his hand and continued to read.

On June first, I stood on the hill next to my house and called out over the orchard, "I will write you into a story! But you must promise to leave me alone. And you cannot hurt anyone!" From the woods came my reply—a flurry of black-winged birds rose into the blue sky like ink bleeding onto blank paper. Their cawing sounded triumphant, like a jeering crowd at a baseball game. I nodded and went inside. At my desk, I opened a new notebook. Using the key, which had supposedly once held shut the gates of Eden, I wrote the first paragraph of what would become The Wish of the Woman in Black.

"In the town of Corglenn, children feared the fall of night. It wasn't the darkness that frightened them—it was sleep. For when they lay in bed and closed their eyes, she watched them."

I wrote for a week straight. The horrible visions finally went away. I woke early in the morning and worked, only breaking for lunch and coffee, until at night, I fell into bed, exhausted. After several chapters, I realized the situation was more complicated than I'd originally imagined. The story was the most terrifying yet—the Woman the most dangerous of all my creatures. Her anger was unrelenting and uncontrollable. I could clearly see where her story was heading. In my mind, I could see the book's last page. The town of Corglenn and everyone in it would be reduced to a lake of quivering sludge. In her story, goodness would not prevail. She would not allow it. Not only would her book be terrible, but if I allowed her to come through the stone child's gate, she would be unstoppable. I knew she would destroy whatever she touched, and she would not stop until Gatesweed, and the world beyond the town's borders, lay in ruins.

Out of the corner of his eye, Eddie saw a shadow moving near the closet door, but when he looked, there was nothing there.

"Eddie!" said Harris. "Don't stop reading!"

"Sorry. I thought I saw . . . ," Eddie started to say. But then he looked down at *The Enigmatic Manuscript.* If he concentrated hard enough, the rest of the room went away. Only the story remained. "Never mind," he said. "Where was I?"

"Ruins," Maggie whispered.

I knew I could not finish writing her story. If I did, I wouldn't be able to face the consequences. Instead, I would have to face her consequences. Unless I could somehow stop her. But how?

Then I thought—if the manuscript allows these creatures to come into our world, I must destroy the manuscript.

I tried erasing it. I tried burning it. I tried soaking it in water, in alcohol, in gasoline. I tried cutting it to pieces. I even tried to scribble over the words using the tip of the pendant itself. But nothing worked—somehow, the magic of the archangel's key had made the pages indestructible, everlasting. I tested my theory with the other manuscripts in my basement, but they were all the same. Permanently marked. Like a stain I could not wash away.

Now that I had stopped putting her story on paper, my visions of the Woman in Black were not confined to my dreams. Everywhere I looked, I could see her, feel her. It seemed that the unfinished manuscript allowed the Woman in Black to appear in Gatesweed, even though the gate was not yet open to her. She could not physically manifest in our world, but it was like I had pulled back the curtain on the window into her world. She enjoyed showing herself to me—reminding me of my promise with the threat of her presence.

"Maybe we were right!" said Maggie. "I think she's still only *looking* at us through the . . . the window, trying to scare us. She can't hurt us. She's *not* real like the other monsters. Not yet anyway."

"So last night," said Eddie, "in my parents' bedroom—"

"It was an illusion," said Maggie. "Just like what happened downstairs a few minutes ago. Harris, your mother didn't see what we saw. The lights in town never really went out. The Woman in Black only made us believe they did."

From the corner of the room came a low moan that slowly crumbled into an angry growl.

"Leave us *alone,*" said Harris, through his teeth.

Eddie refused to look.

Leaning forward, all three of them continued the translation.

It was then I realized I needed a new plan. I was in a mess of my own making. I had been so selfish and needed to fix the situation. Simply putting away my pen would not be enough. If I stopped writing her story, the Woman would drive me into madness and then wait for someone else to finish the job. Since I had started this catastrophe,

I knew I would end it. Rather than wait for her to find me, I would find her.

But first, I needed to open the gate.

It took me a day to figure out how, but once I thought of it, the answer seemed obvious. I would write my own story using the pendant, the same way I had written all of my books. When I finished, the statue would glow blue and the portal would open for me. I would go through the gate, into the dark realm, and put an end to the Woman in Black before she had a chance to follow me home.

Eddie . . ., a voice said from the corner of the room.

Trembling, Eddie tried to ignore everything but *The Enigmatic Manuscript.* As he focused on the book and continued to work, the distractions began to diminish, as if the Woman in Black had no power if he simply didn't acknowledge her presence.

In order for my plan to work, I needed to prepare. As I grasped the silver chain, I was certain that I would not be able to take anything with me—not the book, and most certainly not the pendant.

I knew I needed to write my story, but in leaving it behind, I understood how dangerous the book would be if it fell into the wrong hands. It would act as a set of indestructible instructions, a record of what I had done. Anyone who found and read it would know how to open the gate too. It had been easy enough for me to do it, even unwittingly. And if I failed to destroy the Woman in Black, if she destroyed me first, then there would still be the possibility for her to come through. I decided to write my story in a way that would be difficult to read and leave no evidence. I would need to write the story in code.

Grabbing the pendant, I hastily jotted down a code key in the blank space where I had stopped writing The Wish of the Woman in Black. I opened to the first page of an empty notebook from the local bookstore and drew the chet symbol, as usual. Then, using the new alphabet to translate as I wrote, I began my own story.

Only later did I realize my mistake. In using the pendant to write the code, I'd made it permanent. I knew I'd have to finish quickly, then hide The Wish of the Woman in Black and the code key somewhere no one would ever find it in my absence. A separate place, away from the book containing my own story. I decided to dig a hole underneath a stone in my basement. It seemed appropriate, like a character had done in The Witch's Doom.

After that, I would need to hide my own story and the pendant where they would be protected. The idea for the perfect place came to me from another of my books.

The lake.

If anyone ever came close to the water, just like in The Rumor of the Haunted Nunnery, the dogs would chase him away. The animals would guard my two relics—the pendant and my book. After trying to destroy The Wish of the Woman in Black, I already knew that the water would not hurt my new book's pages. If the pendant eventually became oxidized and rusted, then no one would ever be able to open the gate again, though I doubted such good fortune.

I buried The Wish of the Woman in Black under the stone in my basement. That night, I brought the still-unfinished story of my life, the pendant, a canvas bag, and a metal box with me into the woods.

In the clearing, my flashlight swept across the stone girl's face. Ignoring her, I made my way down the hill toward the lake. The water reflected the stars. I placed the bag onto the shore and reached inside. I pulled out the pendant and the notebook. I turned to the end and began to write. I have been doing so ever since. . . .

I've written everything on the past two pages only moments ago. Here I stand on the edge of this nameless lake in the middle of these nameless woods. I've finally caught up to myself.

When I finish this last paragraph, I will stand up and place the notebook and the pendant into the bag. I will place the bag in the box. After that is done, I will close the box and throw it into the lake as far as my strength will allow. I will watch the box sink. Finally, I will climb the hill toward the clearing where the statue will be waiting, I hope, to let me through. What happens after that is a story for when I return . . . if I return. Even though this isn't over, I must write The End or it won't work. So here goes. . . .

The End.

There was silence.

Finally, Harris said, "But what *did* happen after that?"

"Maybe there's more," said Eddie. "Maybe there's another book."

After typing Nathaniel Olmstead's name into the search engine, he said, "Here. Look." On the screen was the article that Harris had showed Eddie at the beginning of the month. Harris read part of it aloud, " 'When the lake was dredged, police discovered a small metal box. The nature of its contents is being kept secret as the investigation is ongoing. However, an anonymous source has exclusively revealed that this secret evidence has itself mysteriously disappeared.' "

"Oh no," said Maggie. "The book and the pendant were in the box."

Harris nodded. "The police pulled the box out of the lake. If we have *The Enigmatic Manuscript,* that means it's possible that someone else has the pendant."

"Right," said Eddie. "It's only a matter of time before this all happens again to someone else. The Woman in Black is not going to stop until she gets what she wants."

"Unless *we* stop her," said Harris. "Like Nathaniel tried to do."

"But how?" said Maggie.

They sat in silence for a few seconds.

"Maybe the answer is still in *The Enigmatic Manuscript,*" said Eddie. "Could we have missed something?"

Harris's bedroom door swung open, and they all screamed.

Frances stood in the doorway, smiling. "Gosh, you

Harris flashed him a grimace. "There's no other b
Eddie. This is it. The end. He wrote it right here."

"But it's not the end," said Eddie. "We can't give up r
The Woman in Black is still haunting Gatesweed, w
means that Nathaniel didn't succeed."

"Does that mean *we* should try?" said Maggie.

"Of course we should try," said Eddie.

"Hold on a second," said Maggie. "According to
book, the Woman in Black really has no power to harm u
anyone in Gatesweed, right? Other than her being truly cre
what's the real danger of just leaving her alone?"

"The danger," said Eddie, "is the *possibility* of dang
We're talking about the end of the world! If we have
power to stop her, we should do it. She's there, watch
and waiting for someone just like Nathaniel to come alo
so she can use him to do what she wants. As long as s
exists, she's going to want someone to open the stone chil
gate."

"But in order for that to happen," said Maggie, "someo
would need to have the pendant. The one he used to write
of his books. And it's at the bottom of the lake, right?"

Harris and Eddie glanced at each other.

"What's wrong?" said Maggie.

"I guess you should show her," said Eddie.

Harris went over to his desk. He turned on his compute

are jumpy today! Sorry to interrupt," she said, "but soup's on."

Harris groaned, "Mom! You have to stop scaring us like that."

When they finished eating dinner, Eddie, Harris, and Maggie decided to spend the rest of the night thinking about what they'd read.

After everything that had happened, Eddie was frightened to ride home alone, but he knew he needed to be brave. He pedaled as fast as he could, and by the time he made it up the steep road, Eddie was out of breath. He parked his bike in the barn but paused at the walkway that led to the front door. He looked down at Gatesweed. The streetlamps glittered in their concentric circles at the bottom of the hill, like firelight reflecting off ripples in a dark pool of water.

Tonight, a shadow was descending, a gathering darkness, and it was not merely the fallen night. Something sinister is hiding in the corners of this town, and everybody senses it, Eddie thought. They're too scared to acknowledge it. Even if people *could* comprehend what had happened to Nathaniel, Eddie had a feeling they still would keep it a secret.

Harris, Maggie, and Eddie were different. He now understood their responsibility.

Part of him wanted to beg his parents to take him away,

yet something was telling him to stay. He had found his first true friends here. The secret of the stone child had bound them together. They couldn't leave the mystery unsolved. A character in a Nathaniel Olmstead story would never allow that to happen.

The wind tickled his neck and mussed his hair with its cold fingers. Eddie shivered. It was time to go inside.

16

When the phone rang on Saturday morning, Eddie was still in bed. Moments later, his mother knocked on his door.

"It's for you," she said, and handed him the phone.

Eddie sat up and said, "Hello?" Harris was on the other end of the line. He asked Eddie to come apple picking with him and Frances. Eddie had never done anything like that before, but it sounded fun. It would be a pleasant distraction from everything else.

"I thought your mother's store was open today," Eddie said.

"It is," said Harris, "but since we're open later for the reading tonight, my mom thought she'd take the morning off. I heard your mother's gonna read something she wrote. That's so cool!"

"Yeah," said Eddie. "I know."

~

Around noon, Frances and Harris picked him up, and they drove west along Black Ribbon Road. To Eddie's surprise, she turned left into Maggie's driveway. Maggie was waiting for them outside the small house. She wore a long black coat and a red scarf. She ran to the car and got into the backseat, next to Eddie. "Hi, Ms. May. Hi, Eddie," she said. Then she quietly added, "Thanks for inviting me, Harris."

Harris mumbled something that sounded like "You're welcome." As Frances looked over her shoulder and backed out of the driveway, Eddie noticed that she wore a tiny smile.

The apple orchard a few miles north of Gatesweed was much larger than the overgrown one behind Nathaniel Olmstead's house. Together, they picked four big bags of apples, tasting them as they went along. McIntosh were the sweetest—Eddie's favorite. After that, they each chose a pumpkin from the farm stand.

When Frances wandered away to look for mums for the front porch, Eddie, Harris, and Maggie huddled together and sipped on cider.

"Do you think the Woman in Black will go away now that we finished reading *The Enigmatic Manuscript*?" said Maggie.

"Maybe," said Harris. "Unless we figure out what she didn't want us to know."

Before they could continue, Frances waved to them from the counter near the cash register. She needed help carrying the flowers back to her car. Eddie lifted two small plastic buckets filled with burgundy blossoms off the ground and hugged them to his chest. As he carried them to Frances's car, their pungent scent tickled his nose. Harris and Maggie helped him place them into the trunk of the car, unable now to discuss what they were all secretly thinking about.

Back in Gatesweed, they spent the afternoon helping Frances organize the store for the reading. Eddie set up several rows of folding chairs. Upstairs in the kitchen, Maggie helped Frances put together a couple plates filled with cheese and crackers. Harris went through the store with a feather duster, cleaning places that hadn't been touched in weeks.

As they worked into dusk, Eddie half expected the Woman in Black to appear again. Something told him she wasn't through with them yet.

Eventually, a few people showed up for the reading. Eddie thought it was nice that Frances had *some* town support. It was not a large audience, but there were enough people to create a small din. When Eddie saw his own mother and father, he gave them both a big hug. His father wore a tweed jacket and a navy blue tie. His mother wore a simple charcoal-colored dress with a fuzzy red shawl draped across her shoulders.

"Mom, you look pretty," Eddie said as he took a seat next to her. He saved two chairs on the other side for Maggie and Harris.

"Thanks, honey," she said. She tapped her foot on the chair in front of her.

"Are you nervous?"

"A little bit. It's silly, I know—this is a small bookstore in the middle of nowhere," said Mom.

"It's not silly," said Eddie. "I can't wait to hear your story."

"Well, the story isn't quite finished."

"But you're not reading the whole thing, right?" said Eddie.

"No, only the very first part. I'll feel better once I finish. I think I only have a couple pages left. I'd like to be done by tomorrow."

"Wow," said Eddie. "It only took you a month to write a whole book?"

Mom smiled. "What can I say? Since we moved here, I've been feeling inspired!"

A couple minutes later, Frances stood before the audience and thanked everyone for coming. Harris and Maggie sat down next to Eddie. Frances introduced the first reader, who happened to be a substitute teacher at Eddie's school. She read a short poem about her cat. Next came one of the high school students, who read an essay he'd written for his English class. That was followed by an elderly woman who read a picture book about tadpoles that her daughter had written. Eddie didn't listen to a single word. In his head, Nathaniel

Olmstead's story churned around and around, like storm clouds gathering and growing.

Finally, Frances stood up and introduced Eddie's mom. She clenched her husband's hand, then leaned toward Eddie and whispered in his ear, "Wish me luck!" She squeezed past him and made her way up the aisle to the front of the audience.

"Good luck," he whispered back.

She stood beside the table Frances had set up as a podium. In her hands, she held a small notebook. Eddie closed his eyes and leaned forward to pay close attention to his mother's story. Eddie's mother lifted the cover of her notebook and took a deep breath. "The piece I'll be reading is an excerpt from a larger work called *The Dark Mistress's Desire.*" Then she began to read. " 'In the town of Coxglenn, children feared the fall of night. It wasn't the darkness that frightened them—it was sleep. For when they lay in bed and closed their eyes, *she* watched them.' "

Eddie felt his stomach turn to ice. What was going on here?

His mother was reading the story Harris had pulled from the hole in Nathaniel Olmstead's basement earlier that week! She couldn't have written these words, could she? *The Dark Mistress's Desire. The Wish of the Woman in Black.* The titles were eerily similar, but the stories were exactly the same—the descriptions of the town, the main characters, the plot.

Harris reached out and grabbed Eddie's arm. He mouthed the words, *What is she doing?*

Eddie shook his head and tried to ignore him. His heart pounded silently as his mother read the first chapter of her first book to her first audience. He wanted to stand up, to shout for her to stop, to explain herself, but he couldn't do that, of course. Not only would he embarrass himself and his family, but it would bring attention to the fear he felt inside, and it was the fear that frightened him most. He was certain this was the work of the Woman in Black, that she was watching him even now. Was this merely one of the Woman's illusions? Was it possible that Mom was currently reading a different story, but the Woman in Black was making him hear this one?

Eddie almost couldn't stand to listen to the rest, but finally his mother finished. The audience slowly began to applaud. Eddie turned around. Though most of the crowd appeared to be enthusiastic, several people looked upset. He heard someone behind him say, "I think we've got another Nathaniel Olmstead in our midst. . . ." Eddie couldn't tell if it was meant to be a compliment.

The words echoed in his head.

Another Nathaniel Olmstead . . . Another Nathaniel Olmstead . . .

Slowly, the puzzle pieces started to fit together.

He leapt to his feet, stepping past Maggie and Harris into the aisle. Turning around, he waved to them and quietly said, "Follow me." Without waiting for the audience to stop clapping, he made his way through the store, out the door, and onto the front porch. Harris and Maggie were close behind.

Harris shut the door and said, "What the heck is going on? Did you tell your mother about the book we found in Nathaniel's basement? Is that why she wrote all that?"

"No," said Eddie. "I didn't tell her a thing."

"Did she find the book? *The Wish of the Woman in Black*? Did she copy it?" said Harris.

Eddie shook his head.

"So how did she—" Maggie began, but then she interrupted herself, her realization dawning. "Oh my gosh . . ."

"Is someone going to tell me what's happening here?" said Harris.

Eddie cleared his throat. "I think I know the real reason my family moved to Gatesweed."

The door opened and Dad's face appeared. He looked annoyed. "Edgar, come back inside and tell your mother what you thought of her story. She's waiting for you."

Eddie opened his mouth to speak, but words wouldn't come out. He glanced at his friends. Harris nodded toward the door, and Eddie reluctantly followed his father back inside. Harris and Maggie trailed behind him. Mom and Frances stood chatting near the food table. As Eddie approached, Mom turned and smiled at him.

"So what did you think?" she said.

"I'll let you two talk," said Frances, ruffling his hair and wandering off to greet her other customers.

Eddie felt dizzy, but he managed to say, "It was really . . . creepy."

"Thanks," she said. She was hugging her notebook against her chest. "Coming from you, I'll take that as a compliment."

Eddie reached out and touched the cover. "Can I see it?"

"Sure," she said, "but don't read ahead."

Eddie took the notebook from her. He felt Maggie and Harris come up on either side of him. They looked over his shoulder as he opened the cover. What he saw there nearly caused him to drop the book on the floor. He looked again, this time more closely, to make sure he hadn't imagined it.

He hadn't. His mother had drawn the symbol in the middle of the front page, over the title, like Nathaniel Olmstead's handwritten books in his basement.

"Eddie, what's the matter?" said his mother. "You look like you've seen a ghost."

"Why did you draw this here on the first page?" said Eddie, pointing at the symbol. He knew she'd seen it before—in *The Enigmatic Manuscript* the night they'd moved to Gatesweed—but after everything that had happened, it horrified him to see that she had drawn it at the beginning of her notebook too.

"Oh, that thing?" said Mom, almost distracted. "I don't know. It just sort of popped into my head when I picked up the . . ." She didn't finish. She suddenly looked embarrassed.

"When you picked up the what?" said Harris.

Eddie's mother blinked. "When I picked up my pen," she said, "the symbol popped into my head. For some reason, I wrote it down. For luck or something. I didn't really have a reason."

"What kind of pen was it?" said Maggie.

Eddie's mom took a step backward. "I don't know. It was something I found in one of my husband's boxes of antiques," she said. "In fact, I think it was in there with that book I gave you at the beginning of the school year, Edgar." She waved to her husband, who stood several feet behind Eddie. "Honey, didn't we find that pen at the same antiques fair as Edgar's book?"

"Yeah," said Dad. "I think so."

"The pen . . . What does it look like?" said Eddie, his voice rising. He knew he was starting to sound paranoid, but he could barely think, never mind speak.

"It looks like a . . . small silver dagger," said Mom. "It's very pretty. When I hold it, I just . . . *want to write.*" The three kids stared at her. "What's this all about, Eddie?"

"It's nothing," he heard himself say. "Do you still have it?"

"Of course," she said. "It's at home."

"Where?" said Eddie. "Can we see it?"

She looked at him like he was crazy. "Yes, I'll show it to you tomorrow morning. When I've finished my book."

"No!" shouted the three kids together. Mom was so startled she nearly fell backward into the food table.

"Sorry, Mom. Can we see it now?" said Eddie.

"You're being very strange, Eddie," said Dad. He moved a folding chair as he took a step toward his wife.

"I know I'm being strange," said Eddie. "But it's really important."

"Fine," said Mom, exasperated. "We'll be heading out in a few minutes."

After Eddie's parents said goodbye to Frances, they all piled into the blue station wagon. Eddie, Harris, and Maggie squeezed into the backseat.

"I really wish you kids would tell me why you're so upset," said Eddie's mother.

"We're not upset," said Maggie. "We loved your story. We're just curious about . . . how you wrote it. That's all."

"You're curious about a *pen*?" said Eddie's dad.

Harris coughed. "We . . . really like pens."

Eddie nudged Harris in the ribs. His parents weren't stupid. Harris turned red and shrugged.

It was dark by the time they arrived at the Fennicks

house. The kids scrambled out of the car and tried to wait patiently in the living room. Eddie's mom brought her "pen" downstairs, and when she finally handed it to Eddie, he felt a jolt. It was freezing cold. The tip was sharp. And its chain seemed to shimmer like the tail of a comet. It looked and felt just as he imagined it would. The weight of its history was overwhelming.

"Satisfied?" asked Eddie's mother.

"Sure," said Eddie, trying to control the fear in his voice as he headed up the stairs to his bedroom. "Can we borrow it for a second? I want to try something."

"Well . . . ," she said, putting her hands on her hips. "Okay. Just be careful. I *need* it."

"We'll be careful," said Harris, following Eddie.

Upstairs, Eddie ushered his friends into his room, closed the door, and leaned against it.

"Can I see it?" said Harris, sitting at Eddie's desk. Eddie handed the pendant to him. Maggie knelt next to Harris, reached out, and touched it too. "Do you think it's real?" Harris added.

"If it is, then this all finally makes sense," said Maggie.

Eddie leaned over Harris's chair, opened his desk drawer, and pulled out a piece of paper. Harris handed the pendant back. Gripping it like a pen, Eddie pressed it to the paper. Miraculously, a black dot appeared there. Eddie dragged the tip across the paper, drawing a sharp black line from corner to corner. "It's real, all right. Why didn't I realize this before now?" said Eddie, his voice shaking.

"Realize what?" said Harris. "How your mom ended up with this thing?"

"Yes." Eddie took a deep breath. "Remember the box that the search party found in the Nameless Lake? It was supposed to contain *The Enigmatic Manuscript* and the pendant that Nathaniel hid before disappearing?"

Harris nodded.

"The police lost its contents, and somehow the book and the pendant ended up at the Black Hood Antiques Fair." Eddie put the pendant down. He didn't like the way it felt. The cold seemed to be burning his skin. "My parents happened to buy both items. And just like the pendant led Nathaniel Olmstead to Gatesweed, it began to work its magic on my mother. *That's why we moved here.* My mother said so herself. She came looking for inspiration and found it in Gatesweed."

"So your mom's been writing this book since you moved in?" said Harris.

"Yes," said Eddie. "Somehow, the Woman in Black must have gotten her to write the story that Nathaniel Olmstead refused to finish. My mom didn't realize what she was doing. She thought that she'd finally come up with a good idea."

Maggie stood up, crossing her arms. "If your mother

was the hammer he'd brought with him when they'd snuck into Nathaniel Olmstead's house. "Stone breaks if you hit it hard enough," said Eddie. "Doesn't it?"

"Let's hope," said Harris.

"When should we do it?" said Maggie.

"You heard my mother," said Eddie. "She wants to finish her book tonight." The light on the desk began to flicker. They all stared at it for several seconds. Then Eddie added, "So we need to go *now.*"

finishes writing the book, the gate will open. The Wom
Black will be able to come through."

"We can't let that happen," said Harris.

"But how?" said Eddie.

"Tell your mother she has to destroy her manuscript,"
Maggie.

"It won't matter if she destroys the manuscript," said
ris. "First of all, according to Nathaniel Olmstead, it *ca*
destroyed. Second, the Woman in Black has been wa
around since, like, the beginning of time for this to hap
She will just get someone else to write it someday."

"You're right. We can't destroy the manuscript,"
Eddie. He stared at the black line he'd scratched across
paper. He thought about all of Nathaniel's books hidde
his basement—a permanent record of the town's a
legacy. There had to be something they could do to en
"Do you think we can . . . destroy the gate?"

"The gate?" said Maggie.

"The stone child," said Eddie. "In the woods. Maybe
if we destroy the statue, we destroy the gate? That way,
Woman in Black will never be able to come through!"

"That's brilliant!" said Harris.

"But how do we destroy the statue?" said Maggie. "A
cording to the legend, hasn't it existed, like . . . forever?"

Eddie glanced into his open desk drawer. A shape at t
back caught his eye. He reached inside and pulled it out.

17

Since Maggie lived within walking distance of the Olmstead estate, Eddie asked his father if he would drive them all to her house so they could watch a movie. Eddie's father looked like he didn't believe them—especially since, a few minutes earlier, they'd been acting so weird about Mom's "pen"—but he drove them anyway.

Eddie knew his mother planned on using the pendant to finish writing her book, and rather than explain everything and why that might be a bad idea, he'd simply taken it without her noticing. He hoped she wouldn't be too upset with him when he came home again. *If* he came home again.

The journey through the hills was the same as always. The roads went up and down. They twisted and turned. With every dip in the road, with every sighing rise, Eddie's anxiety grew. For some reason, he felt guilty—if he hadn't been interested in Nathaniel Olmstead books, would his mother still have tried to write her own? Then he thought about the pendant she had found, and Eddie tried to convince himself that what had happened was no one's fault. Whoever came into possession of the object would be drawn toward the gate—especially a writer looking for a story to tell, like Nathaniel Olmstead . . . or his mom.

The pendant was dangerous, and he understood now that it seemed to have a life of its own. He could feel the thing almost vibrating at the bottom of his backpack. There was something in its nature that instinctively needed to be near the gate. And it seemed to have a talent for making people do what it wanted.

Dad dropped them off at the end of Maggie's driveway. They waved goodbye and watched until his red brake lights disappeared around the bend, then they walked up the driveway to Maggie's house. Once inside, she led them to a table in the corner of the kitchen.

"What should we bring with us?" she asked.

"I've got the hammer and the pendant in my bag," said Eddie. "We'll definitely need some extra flashlights."

"That's a great idea," said Maggie, getting up and opening the cabinet under the sink. "I think my dad keeps some in here." She pulled out two small plastic flashlights and placed them on the table.

"Nice," said Harris. "We'll need those to keep away the

Watchers. But what else can we use . . . you know . . . in case some of Nathaniel's other monsters are waiting for us?"

"I guess it would be helpful to come up with a list of creatures from his books," said Eddie. "Then we can match them up with whatever the characters used to defeat them. Hopefully, we can find whatever we'll need here in Maggie's house."

"Hopefully," said Maggie.

A few minutes later, they'd put together a list of things to take on their journey into the woods. Wind chimes for the Wendigo. Glass marbles for the weeping spirits. A stapler for the shadow-stalker. An egg timer for the sand-suckers. Chicken bones for the monster lake-dogs. Plus much more. "Who knows if most of these monsters are still hanging out in Gatesweed," said Eddie, "but at least this list will get us started."

"Scavenger hunt!" said Harris, standing up from the table.

"Shhh," Maggie answered. "My parents are upstairs, probably watching television. We don't want them asking any questions. If they see me leave the house again tonight, they'll want to know where I'm going, and they're not going to buy the 'watching a movie at Harris's house' excuse. Just look around, see what you can find, then we'll sneak out."

They quietly went through the kitchen drawers, refrigerator, pantry, and china cabinet in the living room, taking what they thought would be useful. When they had finished,

Eddie's bag was heavy, but he hiked it up on his shoulder and took a deep breath.

"Ready?" said Maggie as they slipped out the front door.

"Ready," said Eddie and Harris.

They crept down Maggie's driveway to the street, then down the hill to Nathaniel Olmstead's estate.

The clouds parted. The full moon emerged. And suddenly the house rose before them, glowing on the barren hillside like a second moon in a second sky.

They parted the vines and crept through the gap in the broken fence. The driveway stretched up the hill. They began the long walk, shining their flashlights into the shadows. Harris kept his eyes forward, Maggie scanned the woods on either side, and Eddie looked over his shoulder at the driveway behind them. That way, they had all directions covered. The moon was so bright that they almost didn't need the flashlights, but they kept them turned on anyway, in case the Watchers were lurking.

Eddie was careful not to look at the house. He almost expected to see the old woman's face in an upstairs window. They crept around back and hesitated only briefly before heading down the hill to the orchard. As they made their way up the next ridge, Eddie couldn't clear the thought of those tall figures in shadowy robes.

At the top of the ridge, a bird fluttered from a nearby branch, and Eddie nearly flew away as well. He thought of those dogs, the gremlin, and the thing his father had struck with the car a month ago. He wondered if coming here was really worth the danger? Then he thought about the Woman in Black being released into the world, and he stopped questioning himself.

He continued to follow Harris and Maggie quietly through the brush. They came down from the ridge, and the entire forest seemed to shudder. Tonight the trees looked different—they were larger, more gnarled, more threatening. The leafy ground seemed to ripple in waves like whitecaps in the ocean, but whenever Eddie looked directly down, it stopped moving. The light shining through the treetops was almost green. Eddie thought it might be an illusion, possibly sent by the Woman in Black to frighten them, but still, it looked so real.

Above them, something rustled through the treetops, scattering leaves and twigs to the forest floor like hail. The three of them froze where they stood. Looking up, Eddie couldn't see anything but the silhouette of the black branches against the starry sky. Wide-eyed, Harris pointed at Eddie's backpack. "Wind chimes," he whispered.

Cautiously, Eddie unzipped his bag. The small cluster of chimes was buried halfway down, underneath a plastic baggie filled with pieces of leftover roasted chicken from Maggie's refrigerator. As he pulled out the chimes, they rang. The noise was especially loud in the surrounding darkness. He tied the string to his belt loop, allowing the chimes to dangle next to his front pocket, where they jingled and jangled with every step.

"Won't that sound draw attention to us?" said Maggie.

"Maybe," said Harris. "But that's better than being snatched up into the sky by a Wendigo, don't you think? Remember the schoolteacher found in the—"

"If he's up there watching us," Eddie interrupted, "the chimes will keep him away. That's why we brought them."

Maggie closed her eyes and shook her head, as if trying to block out a terrifying vision. They kept walking.

A few minutes later, Harris held out his hands, stopping Maggie and Eddie in their tracks. To their left about twenty feet away through the trees, Eddie could see vague movement. Harris swung his flashlight toward the shifting shadows, and several pale faces appeared. "They're here," he whispered. "Keep your lights on them."

The Watchers watched from between the trees, trapped between the shadows and the moonlight—their white heads seeming to hover far above the ground, like balloons. Eddie kept his eyes on the creatures as Maggie and Harris led him forward. Slowly, the three kids continued to make their way through the woods. Eddie trudged over the brush, trying desperately not to trip. Finally, he could no longer see the skull-like faces. He made sure to keep his flashlight shining behind them as they continued their walk, so the creatures could not follow.

Then Harris stopped them again. "We made it," he said.

Ahead, the statue stood, glowing in the moonlight. Her stone arms reached out to them, holding her stone book. Her stone hair reflected the light in the greenish way the rest of the forest had. She looked so innocent, as if she knew no more about the world than Eddie had before moving to Gatesweed. He almost felt guilty for what he was about to do but then reminded himself that she was merely a piece of rock.

They came into the clearing. A bird chattered in a nearby tree. Another bird cawed, and Eddie heard the flapping of wings. He glanced over his shoulder, hoping he wouldn't see those pale faces and the stretched red lips. There was nothing there but shadows and light.

Harris crossed the clearing. He stopped abruptly, and Eddie nearly ran into his shoulder. Maggie came up beside Eddie. The statue stood only a few feet away. Trembling, Eddie placed his bag on the ground, reached inside, and pulled out the hammer. The moonlight glinted off its tarnished metal claw. The weight of the tool was a relief in Eddie's hand—it felt powerful. Everything was happening so quickly. In a few moments, all of this would be over.

But before Eddie could move, the night groaned and the shadows grew. He glanced toward the edge of the clearing, beyond which the slope led downhill to the Nameless Lake. Several pairs of glowing red lights hovered in the darkness like fireflies. Eddie knew they weren't insects—these strange lights were the eyes of the dogs that had crawled from the lake. The animals' harsh growls began to surround them as more and more of their glowing red eyes appeared on all sides of the clearing. Other sounds came from the forest as well—soft slithering sounds, harsh hissing sounds, the sounds of claws dragging through dirt. Though he couldn't see much in the shadows, Eddie imagined all of Nathaniel Olmstead's monsters approaching through the darkness.

"Quick," he whispered. "The chicken bones. In my bag . . ."

Maggie knelt down and pulled the baggie out of Eddie's backpack. "What do I do?"

"Throw them," said Harris.

Maggie opened the baggie, swung her arm up over her head, then tossed the bones as hard as she could into the woods. All pairs of glowing red lights suddenly disappeared as the sound of scrabbling claws rustled farther into the brush. Barking and growling followed as, Eddie imagined, the monster lake-dogs fought over their favorite treat. He knew that the animals would be distracted for only a short time.

From the backpack, Eddie tossed Harris the stapler and Maggie the sack of marbles. Harris immediately bent over and began stapling the shadows of trees that spilled into the moonlit clearing, as if it were possible to pin them to the ground. "Just to be safe," he said. "I hope this works."

"What do I do with these?" Maggie asked, pouring the marbles into the palm of her hand.

"Just drop them," said Harris. "If the weeping spirits are out there in the woods, those will help."

Maggie opened her hand, and the marbles spilled onto the rocky soil at her feet. They immediately began to roll toward the edge of the clearing, glistening as they reflected the moon's greenish light. Maggie gasped and leapt out of their way. The marbles disappeared into the brush. Moments later a strange cry came from the darkness—a harsh, painful wail that Eddie had once tried to imagine as he'd read *The Ghost in the Poet's Mansion.*

Maggie and Harris glanced at each other, then looked back at Eddie. The three of them seemed to come to a silent understanding, so at the same time, they all nodded. They were safe, but who knew for how long? Any number of other nightmares might be out there, watching them. Eddie turned back toward the statue and raised the hammer. He closed his eyes and brought it down on the corner of the stone child's book.

To his surprise, the hammer bounced away from the statue as if he'd hit it with a rubber mallet. When he opened his eyes to see what had happened, his stomach turned.

Nothing had happened. He looked toward his friends, who stood behind him wearing worried expressions.

“Maybe you should try again,” said Harris. He didn’t sound convinced that it would work, but Eddie appreciated his show of almost-enthusiasm.

Eddie turned and raised the hammer again. This time, he aimed for the robe that draped down the statue’s leg. Again, the hammer bounced away as soon as Eddie made contact. He nearly fell to the ground from the ricochet. Wobbling away from the statue, Eddie dropped the hammer in frustration. “What do we do now?” he cried. “We don’t have a lot of time. The creatures won’t stay away forever.”

“Let me try,” said Harris.

Eddie nodded, even though he knew it would probably be useless. Like the pages of Nathaniel’s handwritten books, the stone seemed to be indestructible. No wonder it had not decayed over the course of the millennia—it *could* not. He bent over to pick up the hammer lying near the statue’s base. When he did so, he spotted the carved designs in the pedestal upon which the child stood. Hairy monsters, dragons, sphinxes, and countless other nasty beasts. He had noticed these designs when he’d examined the statue closely that first day Harris had brought him here, and now, in the moonlight, after all he had learned over the past few weeks, they seemed to tell a new story.

“Hold on a second, you guys,” said Eddie, glancing at his friends over his shoulder.

He leaned forward and touched the carvings. Letting his

fingers brush against the images of the mythical beasts, Eddie remembered something he'd read in *The Enigmatic Manuscript.* He inhaled sharply and toppled away from the statue, falling onto his rear end in the dirt.

"What is it?" said Maggie, rushing forward to help him.

Eddie knelt, his head reeling with the possibility that he might have figured out a solution. Reaching inside his backpack, he pulled out the spiral notebook in which he'd written the translated text from *The Enigmatic Manuscript.* He frantically began flipping through the pages. The section he was looking for was somewhere in the middle—where Nathaniel was in Romania, learning about the legend of the key.

"Eddie, what are you doing?" said Harris.

Finally, Eddie found the right page. He held the book close to his face, so he could read the passage aloud. " 'Whenever any creature was refused passage into the Garden, the archangel used the key to carve its image into the stone pedestals as a record of its depravity,' " said Eddie. "Look, you guys." He pointed to the images of the beasts carved into the base of the statue. "These must be the creatures that the angel refused entry to Eden. The angel used the key to mark them into the stone, so he would remember that they were not allowed to pass." He waited for Maggie and Harris to understand, but they only looked confused. "The key is the pendant!" Eddie whispered. "According to the legend, *the key can carve the stone.*"

Harris and Maggie both gasped.

Eddie continued, "And if it can carve the stone, it may be the only way we can actually destroy the gate. Nathaniel Olmstead must not have realized he had the tool to stop the Woman in Black before he went through the gate to confront her himself."

"Quick," said Harris. "Take the pendant out of your bag. See if it works."

Eddie shoved his fist into his bag, but the opening became a mouth filled with small sharp zipper teeth. The backpack began to wiggle and squirm, as if it were filled with rats. Two shiny black buttonlike eyes blinked at him from the small front pocket. The bag's mouth closed on his forearm, and Eddie screamed louder than he had ever screamed in his life. Falling backward into the dust next to the statue, he pushed and kicked the bag away until it was a crumpled, dirty pile of nylon canvas.

"What's wrong with you, Eddie?" said Harris. "Get the pendant!"

"But it was . . . ," said Eddie, staring at his bag, which lay a few feet away. "Alive?" It no longer had eyes or a mouth, only a logo and a zipper.

"What do you mean it was alive?" said Maggie, from behind him.

"It bit me," said Eddie, keeping his eyes on the bag in case it made any sudden movements. What if it was playing dead?

Holding up his forearm, Eddie examined his sleeve. It was intact. He realized that he hadn't actually felt any pain. "Didn't you see?"

"No," said Harris, "I didn't see. I'm a little busy here."

Kneeling in the dust, Eddie turned around. Harris stood behind him, shining his flashlight at the pale faces staring from the shadows at the edge of the clearing. The Watchers had found them again.

"Hurry, Eddie," said Maggie, standing beside Harris, holding her own flashlight against the tall, black-cloaked figures.

Suddenly, Eddie heard a different voice—a deeper voice, a smooth voice, like sweet dark syrup. *Why do you want to hurt me, Eddie?*

He gasped, realizing why his book bag had appeared to attack him. The Woman in Black had created the illusion. She was nearby, watching him through the veil between her world and his. She was trying to stop him. Scrambling toward his book bag, Eddie chanted, "It's not real, it's not real, it's not real. . . ." He looked away from the zipper, took a deep breath, and reached inside. He slid his hand back and forth along the bottom until his fingers finally made contact with cold metal, then he grabbed the chain and yanked it free. The bag began to writhe on the ground beside him, so he quickly kicked it away.

As he scrambled to stand, Eddie noticed that the carvings

on the base of the statue looked different. They were larger than they were before, drawn with more detail. The etching of the dragon now had individual whiskers poking out from the sides of its mouth. The sphinx's wings were constructed of intricately interlaced feathers. Several hairy little creatures seemed to stare at Eddie, their pupils dripping with anger. Hesitantly, Eddie inched forward, and the symbols began to move. They squirmed and pushed against each other, as if there was suddenly not enough space on the stone pedestal to contain them all. Before Eddie was able to back away, the creatures spilled from the statue's base and rolled onto the dusty ground inches from where he stood. The monsters appeared to be made out of stone. They rose to their feet, like little moving statues. His first instinct was to run, but he stopped himself. "This must be an illusion too," he whispered.

Still, he clenched his jaw as the tiny creatures collectively crouched around his ankles. The dragon lowered its head and began to growl as it eyed his shoelaces. Eddie held tight to the pendant and wrapped the silver chain around his wrist. He raised his foot and held it over the small group, threatening the creatures with the sole of his sneaker. Before he could take a step, the monsters leapt into the air. Eddie shrieked and ducked, preparing for the attack, but when none came, he glanced up. The dusty ground around his feet was clear. The monsters were gone!

"Arrgh," Eddie cried through his teeth. "I can't tell what's real and what's not!"

"Don't think," said Maggie, behind him. "Just do it, Eddie!"

Once again, Eddie turned around. His friends were still holding off the Watchers—the beams of their flashlights shaking as the creatures opened their gaping black mouths.

"You wanna switch places?" said Harris.

Eddie shook his head. "No," he whispered. If he didn't do this himself, he was certain he'd never be able to sleep again. He turned around. As he found the courage to take a step toward the statue, he saw a hulking mass of shadow rise up from behind the stone child. The Woman in Black wrapped her arms, almost lovingly, around the girl's neck. Her hideous mouth pulled back into a grotesque smile. The black holes in her face bored into Eddie's chest, and he felt himself almost pushed backward in revulsion. She was closer than ever to coming through the gate—Eddie could feel her presence trying to burrow under his skin.

She began to speak. She sounded tired. *I have many friends, Eddie. My children.* In his head, he heard her voice, each word like a bit of smoke releasing itself from a lick of flame. *You have met some of them, haven't you?* she said, her mouth unmoving. *You will be my friend too, my child. Listen to me. Give me what I want, and when I am through, I will give you anything you want.*

Eddie tried to speak, but he couldn't. *Anything I want?*

What *did* he want? he wondered. What could *she* possibly give to him?

As if in answer to his question, Eddie suddenly found himself thrown into the air. Looking around, he realized he was in a school cafeteria, sitting on the shoulders of two football players. The entire school crowded around him. All of his teachers smiled brightly, and the prettiest cheerleaders chanted his name. Triumphant music began to play as—

Eddie sat on a gold throne in a room made of giant marble pillars that stretched as far as he could see. Enormous platters of food were piled around him—vibrant, colorful fruits, roasted crackling meats, desserts covered in so much whipped cream he could not tell what was underneath. The sweet smell was intoxicating. His mouth watered as—

Eddie flew high over a lush green countryside. Wind whipped at his face. Sunlight poured around him as he raced through the clear blue sky. Looking up, Eddie could see strange wings attached to his back. They appeared to be made of clouds. . . .

Then he was back in the Nameless Woods—the pendant throbbing, ice cold, in his hand.

Anything you want, the Woman repeated.

He glanced at Harris and Maggie—his first real friends—who stood entranced and speechless at the sight of the Woman behind the statue, holding their flashlights against the Watchers at the edge of the clearing. Harris was beside him on his left, fierce courage written on his face. Maggie stood on his right, unflinching determination pulsing behind her eyes.

He remembered the conversation he'd had with Maggie at the beginning of the school year. She had told him, "Epic tales of good and evil are so unnecessary. Those kinds of battles are fought every single day, right here. Kapow." Eddie recalled how she'd pointed at his head and fired her finger like a gun. He finally understood what she meant. Those kinds of battles are fought every single day—right here—inside every decision he made, in order to do what he knew was right.

I don't need you to give me what I want, Eddie thought at the Woman. I've already got what I want standing here beside me.

He clutched the silver pendant in his fist and took a step toward the statue. The Woman rose up, towering over him like night. He stepped forward again just as the statue clearing turned dark. He glanced up. Blocking out the moon, the Woman's face now glowered at him from the sky. He turned away and looked into the stone child's eyes. She seemed to stare knowingly back at him, giving him permission to do what was needed.

Suddenly, the Woman in Black reached down at him with her shadowy hands, her arms stretching from the sky like tar pouring from a cauldron. Eddie cringed as her bony fingers swiped at him, but he felt nothing as her hands passed through him. She couldn't hurt him—not yet, at least. He raced forward, lunging at the statue. Eddie grasped the key tightly. He raised it over his head, paused for only a moment to get the best grip, then plunged it into the stone child's chest. In his head, Eddie heard the Woman scream. The pendant slid into the stone like a key in a door.

The forest instantly went silent—all sounds of wild creatures ceased. Eddie looked around and saw that the three of them stood alone.

The ground trembled. Where Eddie stood, the pebbles rattled like sand on a drum. Eddie turned back to the statue and watched as cracks spread from where the key had pierced it. Without thinking, he reached forward and grabbed the end of the pendant from which the silver chain dangled. Using the heel of his palm, he pushed as hard as he could, and the cracks crept out across the stone child's chest and traveled down her alabaster robes. Dark lines raced across her body—out to her arms, up her neck, to her head, even across the book. Like ink on paper, the lines bled until every inch of her held a crack. Then she started to crumble. Eddie leapt away from her and ran to where Harris and Maggie stood.

They watched as small bits of stone slowly fell away. The statue continued to erode, and after a moment, like a pause before an exhalation, her body simply disintegrated into dust. Moments later, a small breeze came from the direction of the lake and blew most of it away.

After the dust settled, the necklace lay sparkling in the dirt as it caught the moonlight's white reflection. Harris, Eddie, and Maggie watched in awe from the center of the clearing. After a moment, Eddie stepped forward, picked up the necklace from the ground, and slipped it into his backpack.

A voice came from somewhere—it was so quiet, it was impossible to tell exactly whether it was above, below, in front, or behind the three of them. Secretly, Eddie knew it was the Woman in Black, screaming to him as the gate closed to her forever. She said something none of them could hear, and then her voice died away.

Eddie sighed in relief.

"Are you okay?" said Maggie, tucking her hair behind her ears.

"I guess so."

"That was awesome! Nice job, Eddie," said Harris.

Eddie glanced around at the forest. The dogs had disappeared. The Watchers were no longer watching. All the other creatures that might have been hiding in the shadows were gone.

18

They trampled their way back through the woods in the direction of Nathaniel Olmstead's abandoned house. Eddie was exhausted. He knew his friends felt the same way. Each held a flashlight, swinging the light at every snap of a twig or rustle of leaves. Eddie had a feeling he'd be sleeping with the lights on tonight, yet for some reason, he was also certain they didn't need to worry about the monsters anymore. They'd defeated the scariest one of all. Now they simply had to get home.

When they reached the orchard, Eddie heard something that made him want to run all the way up the hill. It sounded as if someone behind them had coughed. Harris and Maggie heard it too. They both spun, holding the flashlights against the shadows between the trees on the hill. But they didn't see anything. Had they imagined the sound? Or was there another monster who had followed them from the clearing?

They had destroyed the gate. Right? They had nothing to worry about.

But as they walked past the last row of twisted apple trees, Eddie heard the distinct sound of feet brushing through the grass behind them. This time, when Eddie spun around, his flashlight found its target.

A pale face stared back at him, squinting as the beam of light shone in its eyes. Eddie's hand shook, and he dropped his flashlight. A man stood ten feet away, backlit by the moon. Even so, Eddie thought he could still make out some of the distinct details of the man's dark face. The eyes had aged since the last photograph Eddie had seen. The beard had grown shaggy and gone gray. His ratty hair now hung past his shoulders. Time had passed since his picture had appeared on a book jacket. Thirteen years, to be precise.

Harris and Maggie spun, their own lights taking over for Eddie's. Eddie bent down to pick up his own from the grass. Then, as they all shone their flashlights on the man who stood behind them, Eddie's friends discovered his identity. They were staring into the eyes of Nathaniel Olmstead.

"Who—who are you kids?" said the man, holding

his hand up to block the blinding light. He wore dingy clothes, a torn T-shirt, and dark, stained pants. An acrid stench surrounded him, as if he hadn't bathed since the last time he'd set foot amongst these overgrown trees.

Eddie couldn't believe what he was seeing. He opened his mouth to talk, but he was so nervous, nothing came out.

Harris spoke up instead. "I'm Harris," he said. "This is Maggie. And this is Eddie." He paused before adding, "Are you Nathaniel Olmstead?"

The man nodded, a hint of skepticism in his eye. "Where are we?" said Nathaniel.

"This is the orchard behind your old house," said Harris. "You're back in Gatesweed."

Nathaniel opened his mouth and looked toward the sky. A wave of relief seemed to wash over him. He dropped to his knees and pressed his palms to his face, clutching his forehead with his long fingers. After a long moment, he shook his head and lowered his hands. "How?" he said. "How?"

The three of them looked at each other. How were they supposed to answer that question? Nathaniel continued to kneel in the grass, staring in disbelief at the hill where his house sat like a sentinel waiting for their approach. The wind blew dead leaves through the field, and the man began to tremble. Eddie stepped forward. He held out his hand to Nathaniel. "Come on," said Eddie. "It's a long story."

~

The four of them made their way up the hill to Nathaniel's house. Once at the back door, Harris, Maggie, and Eddie managed to pull the last of the wooden planks away from the frame. Nathaniel opened the door himself, pausing before going inside. The three of them followed him into the dark kitchen.

They sat at the dining room table, amid the scattered crystals of the fallen chandelier. They rested their flashlights in the middle of the table, the bluish light reflecting off the shards, painting the walls and ceiling with tiny rainbows. "Are you hungry? Thirsty?" Eddie asked Nathaniel. "Can we get you something from the kitchen?"

Nathaniel laughed, a surprising, radiant sound that seemed to brighten the decay around them. "I am hungry and thirsty. But I'm certain my cupboards are currently bare." He began to cough slightly. "How long have I actually been gone?"

"Almost thirteen years," whispered Maggie.

"Wow," said Nathaniel. "Thirteen years." He picked up a shard of crystal from the dining room table. "I have no words."

"Where were you?" said Harris cautiously. "What happened?"

"Ah," said Nathaniel, looking up at them. He turned the shard, end over end, tossing an echo of light across his forehead, as he contemplated his answer. "That too is a long story." He took a deep breath. "So we both have stories to tell. The question is . . . who goes first?"

Eddie, Maggie, and Harris explained everything they had gone through over the past month, starting with Eddie's arrival in Gatesweed and his mother's discovery of *The Enigmatic Manuscript.* Eddie told the stories about encountering the monsters in and around Nathaniel's estate, how they had figured out the code, and finally, their struggle to defeat the Woman in Black. Nathaniel was horrified to hear that both his book and the necklace had been discovered in the Nameless Lake, but he was impressed with the diligence of these three makeshift detectives to solve the mysteries of the strange objects.

When Eddie explained how he had come to destroy the statue in the woods using the pendant, Nathaniel threw the crystal shard he'd been holding against the wall. He hung his head, as if he were trying to hold back some sort of wild emotion. Laughter. Tears. Eddie couldn't tell which.

"Of course!" he said, once he calmed down. "If only I'd had Eddie's foresight thirteen years ago, I never would have made the journey I did."

Nathaniel went on to explain what had happened to him the night he finished writing *The Enigmatic Manuscript* and opened the gate. After he tossed the metal box with the pendant and the book into the Nameless Lake, he watched as the dogs' red eyes began to appear, like he had expected, under the surface of the water. He turned and quickly ran up the hill toward the clearing. When he saw the statue, glowing brilliant blue, his situation, which had once felt like a work of fiction, suddenly became all too real. He paused, wondering if he should go home and face his fate. But then he heard the dogs approaching quickly from the lake. Nathaniel ran toward the stone child. When he reached the statue, the forest disappeared, the world changed, and suddenly he found himself standing in the middle of a dark, muddy field. The sky was filled with charcoal-colored storm clouds. On the horizon, he could see what looked like a deserted, burned-out town. The statue was still beside him, but it no longer glowed. He was alone in an unfamiliar world. Frightened, he reached out and touched the statue, expecting to find himself back in the woods behind his house. But as the stone of the statue cooled the palm of his hand, Nathaniel instantly realized his mistake. The gate had closed. It would not remain open for him to travel back and forth between Gatesweed, as he had assumed it would. And Nathaniel no longer possessed the key with which he could open it.

He spent the next thirteen years—the story of which he insisted could fill countless books—building a life, struggling to survive in the new, impossible landscape, regretting every minute of his decision. The worst part—the Woman in Black was nowhere to be found. Either she was hiding, or she existed in another world entirely—one that Nathaniel knew he would never be able to reach.

Only earlier that evening did things change for him. He awoke from a nap and found himself lying at the edge of a circular clearing in familiar woods. He thought he might have been dreaming—so much of his life had seemed like a dream—but then he heard footsteps tramping through the brush nearby. He got to his feet and followed the sound through the woods and over a small hill. That was moments before Eddie had found Nathaniel in the orchard, blinding him with the flashlight.

"But how did you come back all of a sudden?" said Harris.

Nathaniel thought about that. "I'm not really sure," he said. "All I can think of is that when Eddie destroyed the gate, those who had traveled through it, like me, were pulled back to the world from which they'd originally come."

Eddie leaned forward. "If that's true," he said, the excitement in his voice filling the small room, "that means all the monsters that had come through the stone child's gate must have been sent home too."

"I hope so!" said Maggie.

"That's why we didn't see any monsters in the woods after the statue crumbled," said Harris. "No one in Gatesweed has to worry about them anymore. We're all safe now."

"I don't know how to thank you," said Nathaniel. "I think you kids are brilliant for figuring this out. And very kind for saving someone who, after thirteen years in his own private purgatory, wasn't sure he deserved to be saved anymore."

Eddie blushed. "We wouldn't have been able to do it if we hadn't loved your books so much. Reading them has always been sort of like . . . a lesson . . . in fighting monsters!" He laughed as he heard the words come out of his mouth. They sounded so silly, but ultimately, they were true. Nathaniel's books had been the best preparation for this crazy ordeal.

Nathaniel smiled. "Then I should have known better how to take care of them myself."

After a moment of quiet, Maggie said, "What are you going to do now that you're back?"

"Is that a subtle way of asking me if there will be another book?" said Nathaniel, raising his eyebrow.

Maggie looked flustered for a second. "Of course not," she said. "I only meant . . ." She didn't finish her sentence. As she slumped into her chair, Eddie realized that her question *had* been a subtle way of asking Nathaniel if there would be another book. For someone who had never considered herself to be a fan of scary stories, Maggie certainly looked embarrassed.

"I'm kidding," said Nathaniel, smiling at her. "To answer

your question, though, all I really want to do right now is take a shower. . . . As for the writing . . . I no longer have my *precious* silver pendant." He sounded sarcastic. "Who knows if I'll ever be able to write anything again? To be completely honest . . . I don't really care."

Eddie didn't believe him. He bent over and lifted his bag off the floor. Placing it on the table, he undid the zipper. Very carefully, he reached inside and pulled out the necklace. With the chain wrapped around his fingers, Eddie allowed the pendant to swing slowly as he held his hand above the table.

Nathaniel shook his head. He slowly reached out and took it from him. "I don't *want* it, but if I don't keep it safe, who knows where it will end up next."

Suddenly, Eddie thought of his mom. She was probably frantic, wondering where he was. He was certain she had discovered that he'd taken her "pen." He hoped she wouldn't flip out when he told her he'd "lost" it.

"But it doesn't matter if anyone uses the pendant to write another book. Does it?" said Harris. "The gate is destroyed."

Nathaniel smiled a sad smile. He shook his head. "According to the legend, there were *two* stone children. Weren't there? As long as the other statue exists, someone might use the pendant to try to open the gate again. I think it's our job now to make sure that never happens."

When Eddie heard Nathaniel say that, he felt like

someone had punched him in the stomach. "But where *is* the other statue?" he said.

Nathaniel clenched the silver pendant in his fist and lightly tapped it on the table. "I hope," he said, "we never find out."

[264]

EPILOGUE

Weeks later, on the evening of Halloween, the town green bustled with activity. The first autumn festival in many years had brought people out of the woodwork. Tents open for business lined the perimeter of the lawn. People were selling everything from cotton candy and caramel apples to balloon animals shaped like vampires and werewolves. There were games where contestants had to topple heavy bottles with baseballs to win giant stuffed frogs for their girlfriends. A small Ferris wheel whirred on one of the long stretches of grass near the church. A portable carousel spun at the opposite end of the park, next to the big mill. Its music hummed cheerfully, oblivious, as several people stumbled away from it, green and dizzy. On a banner spanning the front of the white gazebo, someone had painted in bright red the words WELCOME TO DARK TIMES IN GATESWEED. Eddie strolled through the park and thought it all looked beautiful. He wished he could take his time, but he knew there were other matters he needed to attend to.

Standing next to the gazebo were a tall skinny witch and a floating white sheet with legs, which, Eddie assumed, was supposed to be a ghost—Maggie and Harris in costume. They waved as he approached.

Harris shouted, "You're late!" and grabbed Eddie's red sweatshirt sleeve.

"Sorry," said Eddie, laughing as he tripped over his own red shoelaces. He was dressed like a devil. He'd painted his face maroon and glued two latex horns to his forehead. Even though the coming night was brisk, he'd already begun to sweat. He could feel the makeup running down his neck. He pointed over his shoulder to the vendor tents where his parents lolled, looking at some of the crafts the local artisans were selling. "My dad couldn't find a parking spot."

"Excuses, excuses," said Maggie from behind her own bright green face paint. "We're going to be late."

"The reading doesn't start for a half hour!" said Eddie.

"But we need to get good seats," said Harris, stepping into Center Street and making his way toward The Enigmatic Manuscript, which was lit up like a jack-o'-lantern. There was already a crowd at the door, spilling off of the recently painted front porch. People were dressed in costume, scattered across the sidewalk. Eddie could see several news vans parked along the curb; reporters and cameramen leaned against them, as if waiting for something exciting to happen. If Eddie didn't know better, he might have thought that, inside the store, Frances was offering the best treats in Gatesweed.

As Harris pushed his way through the crowd, Eddie heard whispers from behind the crowd's many masks. In the front window, Eddie read the sign that Frances had posted early last week—WELCOME THE RETURN OF NATHANIEL OLMSTEAD. JOIN US ON HALLOWEEN FOR HIS READING OF A NEW STORY, HIS FIRST IN OVER THIRTEEN YEARS!

The crowd continued to push back, until finally, when the three of them made it to the top of the stairs, a blond woman wearing a tutu and pink tights turned around and glared at them. "There's a *line,* you know," she said through her teeth.

Harris blinked at her through the eyeholes cut in the sheet. "This is *my* store," he answered simply. Harris took out his key and held it up for everyone to see. The woman in the tutu shot them all a dirty look but stepped aside.

Eddie chuckled to himself as he squeezed past her and followed Harris and Maggie through the front door of the empty bookstore. Nathaniel Olmstead's diehard fans had come many miles to see him. Who could blame them for being excited?

Inside, Eddie followed Harris and Maggie past rows of

folding chairs to the very front, where big pieces of white paper marked RESERVED were taped to the seats.

"See?" said Eddie. "We're not late at all."

Harris rolled his eyes, but Eddie could tell that his friend was smiling. Each sat down with a satisfied huff. The door in the rear wall of the store opened, and Frances peeked out. When she saw them, she waved. "Oh good," she said, "I was about to start letting people in. Eddie, make sure you save two seats for your parents. Your mother is really excited."

"I will," said Eddie.

A month earlier—on the night he, Harris, and Maggie destroyed the gate in the Nameless Woods—Eddie had come home to find his mother typing at the kitchen table. He expected her to be upset with him for taking the pendant. He wasn't sure how to tell her that she'd never see it again. When he closed the front door, she glanced up, and he realized that she was upset for a different reason.

"Where have you been?" she cried. "We called Maggie's house, and they said you weren't there."

Eddie thought quickly. "We were hanging out outside."

She looked at him skeptically. "How'd you get home?"

"We walked," said Eddie.

"That doesn't sound very safe." She sighed. "How many times do I have to ask you to call?"

"Sorry," said Eddie. "I promise, I will never, ever, ever forget again."

She looked at him strangely, but after a moment, she smiled. "Well . . . I also wanted to tell you my news," she said. "I'm done!"

Eddie felt his face flush, suddenly panicked that his ordeal in the woods had been for nothing. She had finished the Woman's story. Did that mean the gate was now open? "But your pen . . . ," Eddie started to say.

"You can have it," said Mom, getting up from the table and giving him a hug. "I finally realized that it was hard to write with. For some reason, it always made me sort of cold! I'm better off without the darn thing. I just typed the last few pages directly into my laptop. Simple as that."

Eddie heaved a sigh of relief.

"Would you like to read it?" Mom asked.

Frances walked to the front of the bookstore and opened the doors. The costumed fans who had been standing on the front porch poured in. Eddie couldn't help but imagine the gate in the woods as he watched vampires, goblins, pirates, one Frankenstein monster, and several of the living dead crush each other trying to get through the door. He overheard bits and pieces of their many conversations as they filled the empty rows of chairs behind him.

There were the true Olmsteadys: *"I can't believe he's back!"* or *"This is going to rock!"*

There were the skeptics: *"I bet you this was all a publicity stunt to get us to buy a book!"* and *"There's no way this can live up to the hype. . . ."*

And finally, there were the tagalongs: *"Nathaniel who?"*

At the very back of the room, Eddie noticed Mrs. Singh, the librarian, standing next to Wally, the policeman. She whispered something into his ear, then glanced at Eddie suspiciously. On the other side of the room, Eddie recognized Sam, the skinny tow truck driver he'd met the day he'd moved to Gatesweed, leaning against a wall in his leather jacket. He kept his eyes fixed intently on the podium at the front of the room, wearing a curious expression as well.

A couple weeks ago, Nathaniel had assured him that every author has his critics, and every reader is entitled to his or her own opinion. An author simply needs to learn how to deal with all of it, for better or worse. The same could be said about people in general, Nathaniel had commented.

When Mrs. Singh accidentally caught his eye, she looked away, startled. Eddie only smiled to himself, then turned around. Let these people believe whatever they wanted about Nathaniel Olmstead—Eddie knew the truth. He hoped that one day they would too.

"Look. Here he comes," said Maggie, tapping on Eddie's drooping horn to get his attention. Eddie turned around as his parents snuck through the hushed crowd and took their seats next to him.

The storage-room door swung open to reveal a massive

shadowy figure standing in the darkness of the closet. The audience gasped. The shadow stepped forward into the orange light of the bookstore. A black velvet cloak covered the figure from head to toe. Its hem slithered on the ground as the shadow continued to lurch toward the rapt audience. It paused at the podium, seeming to catch its breath for a moment, until it suddenly whipped the cloak away.

Nathaniel Olmstead stood before his audience as they leapt to their feet and burst into tremendous applause. Camera flashes popped, filling the room with a strange, almost constant stream of white light. Under the cloak, he wore a navy blue wool sweater and a corduroy jacket. He'd cut his hair and trimmed his beard. His slight smile was filled with enormous gratitude. He didn't look so very different from the picture on the back of his books. Nathaniel waited several seconds before taking a bow.

Eddie, Harris, and Maggie leapt to their feet as well. Eddie clapped so hard, his hands hurt. He felt dizzy when Nathaniel finally turned to the three of them and gave them a sly wink.

The past two months had been like a dream—at first a nightmare but now a fantasy beyond anything he could have imagined. Over the past few weeks, he and his friends had visited Nathaniel Olmstead several times as the author began to reconnect to Gatesweed and beyond. They helped him clean up the mess that was his house, they brought him groceries and such until he managed to buy a new car, and they kept him company after school when he was afraid to be alone. Once upon a time, Eddie had known what that felt like, and he was happy to be of assistance. Eddie couldn't believe that he could now call his favorite author his friend.

During visits to Nathaniel's house, the four often theorized answers to some of the questions they still had about the Woman in Black and the statue in the woods. For example, was she a particularly nasty member of the Lilim or was she actually Lilith herself? Was she really as powerful as she'd have them believe? Harris wondered why the Woman in Black didn't just have one of the creatures use the pendant to write her story? Nathaniel was certain that none of the creatures would have been capable of such a feat. As cunning and clever as some of the monsters had appeared to be, none of them had ever been thoughtful enough to create something from nothing. To actually write a story, the author explained, is purely a human talent.

After a few weeks, the four of them had become certain that when it came to the Woman in Black, there would always be mystery. These uncertainties, Nathaniel explained, were what made the villains in books so enigmatic and frightening.

Shortly before Halloween, Nathaniel had asked the three friends to accompany him on a walk into the Nameless

Woods. They made their way up the ridge and down into the forest. They passed through the empty clearing where the statue had once stood. The sun hung low in the sky as they hiked toward the lake. Harris, Maggie, and Eddie watched from a distance as Nathaniel plucked a pebble from the shore and tossed it at the glassy water. After a few minutes, the ripples disappeared. The lake was still, reflecting the clear blue sky overhead.

Nathaniel turned around and smiled. "Just to be sure," he whispered.

The crowd in the bookstore roared.

Finally, the author was forced to hold up his hands so the audience would sit down and listen. He waited a few more seconds until the room was totally quiet, then he said, "Welcome. Happy Halloween. Thank you all so much for coming. I can't tell you how pleased I am to see your . . . *horrific* faces."

The audience laughed. Nathaniel merely smirked and picked up a pile of loose papers from the table. "Contrary to reports you might have read in the news, I have not spent the past thirteen years writing a large novel," he said. "Since I have always struggled to come up with interesting ideas, tales of epic proportions have never been my cup of tea. But since I returned to Gatesweed nearly a month ago, I have had the privilege of meeting three amazing people who've not only rescued me from an exile of my own making, but who've also inspired me with their story."

Eddie felt Harris poke him in the arm. Eddie couldn't keep from smiling.

Nathaniel continued, "With their permission, I have begun working on a new book, based on their own recent experiences." The audience gave another round of excited applause. "It is unfinished. I cannot promise that everything I read to you is true. I am a fiction writer, after all . . . but that's not to say this story is a lie. All I can truly promise is a jolt or two, which, I believe, is all anyone really needs in order to remember he's still alive."

Nathaniel did not bother explaining to his first audience in over thirteen years that he used to write all of his books by hand. Only Eddie, Harris, and Maggie knew that after so many years, Nathaniel had a good reason to stop working that way. Since returning to Gatesweed, Nathaniel had purchased a computer for himself. Having recently buried his formerly favorite writing implement under a stone in his secret basement, like Eddie's mother he'd decided to entirely type his stories instead.

These writers would be fine, Eddie knew. With a stone child or without, he had a feeling Gatesweed would always provide inspiration to anyone looking for it.

"Now, without further ado, I present to you *The Secret of the Stone Child.*" With a small bow, Nathaniel began. " 'The blue station wagon had just come around a sharp bend in the road when the creature stepped out of the woods,' " he read. " 'Eddie was the first to see it—a blur of black hair and four long, thin legs. It looked at him with red-rimmed yellow eyes and a gaping mouth full of sharp teeth. "Watch out!" Eddie cried from the backseat.' "

Sitting in the front row, Eddie closed his eyes and listened to Nathaniel's story, his heart racing as he tried to picture what in the world would happen next. Secretly he knew, of course, but he could not admit it to himself. A true fan would never peek ahead to the end of a Nathaniel Olmstead book.

ACKNOWLEDGMENTS

The Stone Child's journey to publication was long and twisted, and she might have been left somewhere along the road but for the support of several amazing people who eventually conjured her to life.

My writing group—Nico Medina, Billy Merrell, Jack Lienke, and Nick Eliopulos—supported and challenged this story, while giving me an excuse to eat bowls of endless pasta, salad, and breadsticks in the middle of Times Square. Thank you, Nick, for seeing "potential" in those first eighty pages, and for placing the unfinished manuscript into nurturing hands. This story really would not have been written without your help.

Through many drafts, my exceptional editor, Jim Thomas, continually picked me up by the scruff of my neck and plopped me back onto that somewhat overgrown forest trail whenever I lost my way in the darkness. Thanks also to Whitney Stahlberg, who, during the final round, provided her own invaluable perspective and direction.

For thoughtful early advice and conversation, I give great thanks to David Levithan, Brian Selznick, Rachel Cohn, and Joy Peskin. For finalizing the small print, thank you, Noel Silverman. The excitement and insight of my first-draft readers—Emily Poblocki, Kathy Gersing, Nic DeStefano, Joanna Ouellette, Josh Chaplin, and Greg Emetaz—is much appreciated. For enthusiasm and encouragement throughout various parts of this writing process, I must also thank Charles Beyer, Brendan Poblocki, Matthew Sawicki, Jack Martin, Andrew Begg, Scott Bodenner, Gary Graham, E. V. Day, Ted Lee, Leon Gersing, Caroline Fairchild, Donna Kay, Gail Roe, Bruce Roe, John Poblocki, and Maria Giella-Poblocki. Like the folks I've already mentioned, you have each made this experience so much easier that I wish I could invent a perfect word to fully express how much your support has meant to me. If ever I do, I'll be sure to whisper it to you in secret.

Finally, I owe a great debt to my favorite childhood authors, whose books still keep me busy reading (and dreaming) late into the night. I am certain their stories shall continue inspiring, enchanting, and terrifying future generations.

DAN POBLOCKI grew up in Rhode Island and New Jersey and currently lives atop a tower in a magical place called Brooklyn, New York. He has always loved telling stories. Beginning in fifth grade, he gathered his friends after school, frightening them with tales of ghosts, monsters, and spooky places. When the author's mother began to receive phone calls from neighborhood parents, warning that her son's stories were giving their children nightmares, Dan decided to write the stories down instead.

The author requests that if *The Stone Child*, his first book, gives *you* nightmares, please refrain from contacting his mother, as she's already heard enough complaints. Instead, you should visit his Web site, danpoblocki.com, where he may offer full apologies, as well as helpful advice for battling your own neighborhood monsters.